SOUTHERN CHARM SOCIETY

KELLY UTT

2022 Standards of Starlight Paperback Edition

www.standardsofstarlight.com

ISBN: 978-1-952893-17-9

Cover art by Elizabeth Mackey

THE DUST

1

REGRETS

RUTHIE

Nashville

In a boxy white house on a windy hill, I lay dying.

It's springtime in Nashville and my impatiens are blooming. I seriously doubt I'll outlast them, come fall. By the time the air turns crisp and frost covers the ground, I will most likely be underneath it, my flesh and bone no longer of use to anyone but the worms.

It's a jarring, sobering thought. *I know. Believe me, I know.* But it's one I can't seem to escape. The time for avoidance has long passed. My life, now, is about my regrets and the days I have left to fix what I've done. My time is running out. I'm not sure what's possible any more.

"Dahlia, darling," I say from my bed, "would you be a dear and bring me a glass of water?"

My mouth is perpetually dry these days. It's a side effect of all the medications.

"Sure!" she chirps politely from the next room. "Be right there, in a jiffy."

The old-fashioned phrase is for my benefit. She says things like that because she thinks it makes me happy. I suppose it does. It reminds me of my formative years and the phrases my dad used. Long ago, I lost track of the way the kids talk these days. I couldn't keep up with them if I tried. Good thing I have no desire to. Not really.

"Thank you," I reply, just as the phone rings. It's a rotary, landline phone that sits on a stand in the grand entrance at the front of my home, not far from my bedroom. A relic handed down from my parents. "Actually, dear, would you get that damn phone?" I ask, amending my last request.

"Right away," the young woman says. I hear her scramble to the foyer, her low heels tapping against the porcelain tile.

I feel guilty having someone as bright and talented as Dahlia care for me like this. She should be back at the office designing fabulous interiors for our clients, not here bringing me water and changing my soiled bed sheets. "You're the best!" I call, working hard to speak loud enough that my voice carries. "I appreciate you."

"Happy to help!" she replies. The phone quiets mid-ring and I know she's picked up the receiver. "Hello, Flores residence. Dahlia Jackson speaking."

I listen carefully, hanging on every word. I purse my lips and slump lower in my bed. I'm fairly certain I know who is calling. I don't want to talk to him. Not really.

"Um hmm," Dahlia says politely into the phone. "I see. Yes, I understand, sir, but you need to——"

He cut her off, as usual. *The asshole.*

"I'm not here," I mumble, hoping she'll read my mind.

I don't get many phone calls anymore. I fully admit that's because I've isolated myself in this house. I have people who would call and visit, if they knew how sick I was. I often think I should tell them. But I never get up the nerve.

It's embarrassing to be so vulnerable. So helpless. I'm a shadow of my former self, and frankly, I don't want to be seen like this. I hung my career on making things beautiful. How can I face the world now that beauty drains from my life like a leaky faucet? The reservoir will soon run completely dry.

"Sir, I can ask," Dahlia says, "But I don't expect her —" There's a pause, then she adds, "fine. Hold on."

"Ugh," I grumble, tugging on a few strands of my thick silver hair. The move is purposeful, as if there's a lever somewhere in my head that will erase the people and situations I don't like if I simply pull it the proper way.

I hear a soft thud as Dahlia puts the receiver down on the wooden table next to the phone. I listen as her heels clink again. This time they're heading my way. "Ruthie?" she asks as she peeks in the door.

I lift the sheet and cover my face. Maybe if she can't see me, she won't ask me to talk to him.

It's silly. I'm aware. Something about facing your own death makes you sillier. At least, it does for me. Who cares what others think? Social norms are quickly becoming irrelevant.

Dahlia's feet arrive at a stop and she sighs. "Ruthie, dear, I'll tell him whatever you want, but you can't avoid him forever."

"Can too," I say.

"You can *not*," she replies emphatically. "You hired him. He's just doing what you asked. What you begged, if memory serves me right."

Now it's my turn to sigh. She's right, of course, but I'm so sick and tired of the whole drama. Mitch Weller can't fix the broken relationship with my daughter. I'm not sure why I ever thought he could. I must have been in denial. One of the stages of grief, if I understand the hospice people correctly.

"I don't want to talk," I say. "Not today."

Dahlia leans against the side of my bed and reaches out for my hand. "What day then?" she asks as I take her palm in mine. "You tell me when, and I'll make sure he accommodates your schedule. Just remember that time is of the essence. Those were the words you used."

"What schedule?" I ask. "We both know I've got nothing to do but die."

I lower the sheet and quickly make eye contact, but I don't hold it. I stare across the room at the framed pictures on the shelves. There are at least a dozen there, all of Meredith and me. Some have Pete in them, too, but there isn't a single one without my Meredith. "She was the most delightful little girl," I say softly.

Dahlia follows my gaze. "Absolutely," she agrees. "I can tell. I understand why you want to reconcile with her, before it's too late. I'd want the same."

I shift in bed and attempt to change the subject. "Say, the year is well underway and we haven't properly discussed Pantone colors. What's Colour of the Year again? We must be sure we're keeping tabs on elements of Southern charm. It's kind of my thing."

The new "it" color is usually announced in early December, and it's true that Dahlia and I haven't given this year's hue the attention it deserves. I used to love talking about the most popular colors and how to incorporate them into our upcoming interior design projects. Here in Nashville, we tend to favor shades of blue.

She thwarts my attempt. Dahlia is a clever young woman. Too clever to fall for my tricks. "There's still time," she says, eyeing my daughter's face in the framed photos. "I believe you can make things right."

I shake my head. "There's not. It's too late for us. For me."

I'm wallowing in self pity. I know it. Dahlia knows it. Even Mitch—on the phone in the other room—probably knows it. It isn't helpful. Can I truly be held accountable for my less than stellar attitude, though? What kind of behavior is expected of dying people?

Dahlia shrugs, her brown skin shimmering in the early morning light that's easing its way through the bedroom window. She's dressed for a day at the office, even though she'll spend all day here with me. I don't deserve such kindness. "As long as there's breath in your lungs, Ms. Ruthie," she reiterates, "there's time."

She's said it again and again, like a broken record. I suppose it's one I need to hear.

She places my hand down gently onto my lap, then turns and walks to the book shelves. There are plenty of books there, tucked beneath the picture frames. For a moment, I'm not sure which she's after.

"You don't have to comfort me," I say, a tear forming

in my eye. "You don't have to do any of this, for that matter. You don't even have to be here right now. Go back to the office. You can handle yourself there without me. You're perfectly capable and competent. I'm just dragging you down at this point."

"Nonsense," Dahlia replies.

"Okay," I add, persistently, "then go home to Rae. Your girlfriend surely needs you more than I do."

She shrugs. "Rae understands what I'm doing here. She supports this fully. If I went home, she'd send me right back. You know that. Besides, you're on a mission that I intend to help you see through. Isn't that what we talked about? Isn't that what I promised?"

I want to ask her what she's doing here. What Rae thinks she's doing here. I don't. I need Dahlia's help, no matter how much I wish I didn't.

No amount of wishing will make my failing heart work again. Doctors have done all they can. The medications I take simply delay the inevitable, and from what I understand, not by long. I'm *really* going to die. Not in the way that every living person is—someday. For me, it's an active process. I'm moving toward death with the momentum of a freight train barreling downhill. One with burnt up breaks that do nothing but spark and scream against their perilous fate.

Dahlia glances into the hallway, a reminder that Mitch is still on the phone, waiting.

"If I talk to him," I begin, "what good will it do?"

I'm doubting my decision to contact him in the first place. What was I thinking, dredging up all that complicated history?

She reaches for one of the framed photos of my daughter. From the confines of a shiny silver frame, Meredith's dimples stare out at me.

"How old was she here?" Dahlia asks as she runs a neat finger across the little girl's cheeks.

My brows raise and the corners of my mouth turn upward into a smile. Remembering the good old days when my only child still loved me will raise my spirits every time. "Six," I reply. "She had just turned six a few weeks prior."

"Such a fun age," Dahlia muses.

I nod. "It sure was. The photo was taken at Opryland, back when it was a theme park instead of a shopping mall." I prop myself up in the bed, rolling onto one elbow. Blood rushes in my ears, then pounds angrily. "Do you remember that, dear? Did you ever go to Opryland?"

Dahlia laughs gently. "I'm afraid not. That place was torn down before I was born."

"Wow," I say. "That's right. I really am old."

"Not old," Dahlia assures me. "You're just … seasoned. That's all."

She smiles broadly. It's the kind of smile that lights up a room. Her genuine rapport is a true gift. How lucky I am to have her in my life. Without a daughter of my own to spend time with, a friend like Dahlia is the next best thing.

"Whatever you say," I reply, my shoulders easing back against the bed. The moment has passed. My enthusiasm has waned. It seems I can only stay excited for a few minutes at a time before my cranky heart puts the kibosh on the whole thing. It's hard to do much that's useful when you have a bad ticker. "Come here," I urge, gesturing with two fingers. "Bring the photo. Sit beside me."

She obliges. She hands me the frame, then sits on my bed and tucks her skirt against the sides of her legs. When I don't speak for a while, she inquires. "Tell me more about that happy little girl."

I yelp, the emotion surprising me. It does that a lot lately, building in my throat and bursting up and out of my mouth. I can't seem to control it. "I'm sorry," I say, lifting a hand to cover my face.

"For what?" Dahlia asks.

"For … I don't know. Everything."

"Stop it," she says, then she takes my hand in hers once again. "Tell me about your daughter on that day, at the Opryland theme park. She looks so content."

I glance down at our hands. Hers young, brown, and strong. Mine pale, gnarly, and wasting away before my very eyes.

It strikes me that this young woman has been alive roughly the same amount of time as Pete has been gone. Dahlia is a living, breathing representation of all the life Pete never got to live. In fact, she has nearly the exact same skin tone. To a casual observer, she could be his daughter. The thought pains me, and I wince. I'm responsible for his life being cut short.

"Ruthie, please," Dahlia says. "Focus on your daughter. Tell me about the day you took this photo. You did take it, right?"

"Actually, Pete did," I reply. "I miss him just as much as I miss Meredith."

"Aw, I know you do, dear," she says sweetly. "He was

your husband. Your great love of a lifetime. Tell me about it. I love hearing your family stories."

I exhale and close my eyes, allowing myself to remember. Within seconds, it feels like I'm back there again, the hot sun burning our shoulders as the smell of freshly-baked funnel cake wafts through the air. Cheerful yells rise and fall in the distance along with the theme park rides. "I held her little hand in mine," I say. "We had ridden an indoor roller coaster called Chaos. Pete was creeped out by the idea of a roller coaster in the dark, so Meredith and I went by ourselves."

"Not sure I blame Pete," Dahlia says with a chuckle. "It sounds pretty creepy."

I wave a hand in the air, keeping my eyes closed. "Nah, it's fine," I reply. "Nothing to worry about. Meredith wasn't scared. Although, I'd thought she might be."

"Atta girl," Dahlia whispers, as if her words of encouragement can reach Meredith's ears.

"When we were in line, inside the building," I continue, my eyes still closed, "there were ticking clocks everywhere. Like, dramatic ticking that got louder the longer it went on. And a voice kept saying over and over again that our time was running out."

Your time is running out.

"Now that's definitely creepy," Dahlia replies. "Pete knew what he was doing staying out of there."

"Maybe so," I say. I open my eyes briefly to share in the fun. My muscles relax as feel-good endorphins flood my bloodstream.

"See, look at you," she coos. "You're positively

glowing, Ruthie. Your daughter has that effect on you. You should talk about her more often."

I nod. "Pete too."

"Pete too."

I turn toward the open doorway. "I don't hear the howler tone, so I guess Mitch is still waiting on the line. I suppose he owes me that much. You know, because of who he is to me."

She nods her agreement. "He'll wait."

Now I know for sure it's him. I adjust myself in the bed and move my head slowly from side to side. I consider Mitch and what he'll say if I give him the chance.

"I'm telling you, I'm not ready," I reiterate to Dahlia. She doesn't skip a beat. She redirects me artfully. Instead of a designer, maybe she should be a therapist. Or a preschool teacher.

"Were you afraid in that creepy roller coaster line?" she asks. "I assume if you were, you didn't let on to Meredith. I suspect a good mom would hide their own fear from the kid in that situation. You were a good mom. Right, Ruthie?"

I jump right back into the memory, feeling the sensory cues as I close my eyes. "No way did I let on," I say. "I was with my girl. I'd climb mountains for her. Hell, I'd move mountains for her. I'd do anything—"

"What did you do for her that day?" Dahlia asks. "When that photo was taken."

"That's just it," I reply. "All I did was ride a roller coaster with her. I held her hand, and I put my arms around her small shoulders to make sure she felt safe as the car wound its way up the circular track and then came zooming down. When we stepped off the ride and back onto solid ground, she flashed me the biggest smile. She was still beaming—skipping even—as we exited the building near where Pete was waiting for us. We paused when we reached him, and he snapped the shot."

"Easy peasy," she replies.

My eyes shoot open. "If only things were that easy now."

Dahlia exhales softly. "Have a little faith," she says. "I know you can't hold Pete's hand, but I want you to hold your daughter's again one day."

Tears spring to my eyes. "I'd love that, but I don't think it will happen. It would have to be a day very soon. There's so much to overcome and very little time. You're sweet to wish for a reunion on my behalf, though."

She pauses, and I get the idea she's deciding whether or not to share something with me. She furrows her brow, her worry evident.

"What is it?" I ask.

"Nothing," Dahlia says quickly, turning away from me. "It's nothing."

I sit all the way up in bed. It takes a lot of effort and my heart skips a beat, but I don't care. I mean to find out what has Dahlia acting strangely. "It's something. I know you better than you might think, young lady. *Tell me*."

Dahlia shakes her head. "It isn't my place," she insists. "Not mine to tell. But if you'd talk to Mitch—"

Suddenly understanding the urgency, I raise a finger and cut her off mid-sentence. My eyes grow wide in anticipation. They meet Dahlia's, and we exchange a knowing look. I can tell this is something big. Something worth facing my fears for. "I'll talk to him. Bring me the phone," I say.

Her face lights up. "Are you sure?" she asks. "You're ready to talk? All of a sudden?"

I nod, then I steel myself for the inevitable.

I haven't spoken to Meredith in many years. Whatever Mitch might have found in his role as a private investigator is unlikely to help mend our relationship. I don't want to get my hopes up for nothing. At the same time, though, I'm desperate to make amends before I die. I allow myself to consider the possibility of unexpected joy entering what's left of my life. Maybe I can still find a way to fix this. Maybe there's a reason out there that would prompt my daughter to forgive, though I wouldn't expect her to forget.

Could it be what I think? The way Dahlia reacted to my story about six-year-old Meredith … the way she picked up that frame instead of any of the others … I have ideas, but I'm not sure I dare say them out loud.

Dahlia goes to the foyer and fetches the phone, its gray cord stretching down the hall and into my room. She holds the receiver in one hand and the base in the other. The way she grins, you'd think she was handing me a winning lottery ticket. Maybe she is.

I clutch the receiver and place it gingerly against my ear. I take a long, deep breath, then ask, "Mitch, my old friend, what've you got?"

2

NEEDLES AND PINS

MEREDITH

New Orleans

"Someone has been watching us," Rosemarie says as she kicks her leg against the supports of the bar stool. "From across the street, by the lake."

"What the fuck?" I ask as I scramble six eggs in a mixing bowl. The sun is just beginning to peek above the horizon. Soft pink light rises outside our kitchen window. "I doubt it's anything to be concerned about. Probably just some tourists admiring the place. It is pretty, if I do say so myself."

"Or maybe they like our dogs," Silas adds without looking up from his laptop.

This makes Rosemarie giggle. She's a dog person. At fourteen, she already has a remarkable way with animals. She insists she'll be a vet when she grows up. Or a dog trainer.

Silas' statement makes sense. Our metal fence stretches to the front edge of the yard, and our dogs like to poke their heads out and greet passers-by. That is, if they aren't lounging on our front porch, which is in plain view. When we're home, they're usually outside.

"Maybe," Rosemarie says to her dad. "If not, I'll bet Mom could run the man off with her foul language. Right, Mom?" A smirk crosses her face.

To that, Silas raises a brow and looks up. He doesn't have to say anything. Our girl is fourteen going on forty. Sometimes, I think she's actually more mature than me.

"I know. I know," I mutter.

Bacon sizzles as I slide the eggs into a skillet then pop three slices of grainy bread into the toaster.

I enjoy cooking for my family. It's a lost art, if you ask me. Especially amongst our well-to-do friends. Many of them have personal chefs, or else they eat out most of the time. When Rosemarie was born, I knew I wanted a more hands-on approach. Silas agrees. At least, he doesn't disagree. He usually goes along with what I want.

My husband closes his laptop and turns to face our daughter. His strong features move as he tenses his jaw, the rich brown skin on his face tightening with concern. He's a remarkably handsome man. "No joke, though. Who did you see out there?" he asks.

She tilts her head to one side and twirls a few strands of dark curly hair—she got that from her father—with her fingers. "Just some man."

"Okay," Silas replies earnestly, without a hint of disbelief. He's a good dad. He waits for Rosemarie to elaborate. Soon enough, she does.

"An old white man. In a silver car. He smokes a lot," she explains, her leg still kicking.

I listen as I grab plates from a cabinet and walk them to our breakfast table around the corner. If Rosemarie has a story to tell, I'd be wise to let Silas get it out of her. I don't comment, but rather let their conversation unfold naturally.

Those two are like peas in a pod. Sometimes, I think I gave birth to Rosemarie simply because she and Silas belong together. I often feel like an afterthought in my daughter's life. Although, granted, maybe karma is dishing up what I deserve in that regard. I'm pretty sure I gave my mom a hard time when I was Rosemarie's age.

I bristle at the thought of my selfish, difficult mother. Our relationship is knotty—er, it was knotty. I put a permanent end to that dysfunctional mess when Rosemarie was born.

"Lots of old men enjoy Lake Pontchartrain," Silas replies considerately, placing a hand on her arm. "What makes you, my darling daughter, think this one is of any particular interest?"

"Like I told you," she says, frustrated. "He watches us."

"Not just our cute dogs?"

"No, Daddy, I don't think so," Rosemarie replies. "They are very cute dogs, but I think he's watching *us*."

Silas stands and walks to the row of windows on the front of the house. He gestures for our daughter to follow. "Is he here now? Show me," he says as he crosses his strong arms over his chest.

"I don't think he comes this early," she explains.

I mind my business, filling three glasses with orange juice and setting the table with silverware and linens. I grab a small vase and step out the back door to cut a rose from our garden. When I return, my husband and our daughter are deep in conversation, both peering out a window as Alphie, our Irish Wolfhound, traipses lazily around their feet. Sara, our chocolate lab, and Calliope, our English setter, are snoozing on their soft beds in the living room. It's too early for either of them to be bothered. I expect they will both perk up once the scent of bacon arrives at their snouts.

"Maybe he's taking a break," Rosemarie says. "I haven't seen him for a few days."

Silas wraps an arm around her shoulders as they stare out at the lake. "What made you decide to wait until today to tell us? Your mom and I are always here to listen when something is on your mind."

"Not always," she replies, too soon for my comfort. "You're at work a lot. Mom too, and she doesn't always listen, anyway. I'm here alone."

My face falls. I hate hearing her say that. "Things are beginning to slow down for me," I interject. "I'm hiring a new designer for our North Shore office to lighten my load. And Dad will have more free time as soon as the hotel opens in Covington."

"Until you get busy with more clients again and Daddy has to open another hotel," she says wistfully. "It's always something. You two are married to your businesses more than you are to each other. I just wish we could spend time together. As a family."

I skip over the last part in my mind. It's the discrepancy between Rosemarie calling him Daddy versus simply Dad that is most uncomfortable. She calls me Mom, after all. Not Mommy. Not anymore.

Maybe subconsciously, I want to minimize the closeness between Silas and Rosemarie. *Of course*, I want my daughter and her father—my husband—to be close. But a part of me still misses my own dad and the closeness we once had. He's been gone nearly twenty years. His absence still stings. Especially because it didn't have to be that way. He didn't have to die. His death could have been prevented.

Silas is silent, so I fill the void.

"We work hard because we want a good life for you," I say to our daughter. "It costs a lot to pay for this house on the lake, with all these bedrooms, and a swimming pool. You enjoy having friends over and entertaining as much as your dad and I do, right? Money doesn't grow on trees."

My stomach turns as I hear the words coming out of my mouth. My mother used to say bullshit like that to me. Like she was so burdened by my existence and how much I'd cost her. I swore I'd be different. I *am* different in many ways. In others, I'm not different enough.

Silas knows my triggers. He sees my distress and jumps in. He's a good man.

"What your mother is trying to say is that we want to spend more time with you, too, kiddo. The time we have together is the best. Don't you think so?" He pulls her into a playful headlock and kisses her silky hair.

"Right," I manage. "What your dad said." I set a plate of bacon and eggs on the breakfast table, then join for a group hug. "I love you, Rosemarie," I say. "You're my baby girl."

"I'm not a baby," she says, but she smiles, accepting the apology I didn't actually articulate.

A swirl of mixed emotions moves through me. I know I have issues left over from a troubled childhood. As Rosemarie gets older, they seem to be rearing their ugly heads. Having a teenage daughter is like having a mirror in my face all the time, reflecting back the parts of myself that I'd rather keep hidden. Silas doesn't have the same burden. He's free and easy, in that regard. But she's right. We're away too much. We should spend more time together. We'll never get these years back.

She pulls away, and I continue prepping for breakfast.

When everything is on the table, we sit down together and break bread. Silas and I eye each other cautiously as we salt eggs and slather preserves on toast. We need to know more about the man Rosemarie saw. At the same time, we don't want to overreact and cause her to clam up. This thing about a stranger watching us is, potentially, a serious concern. So is navigating the relationship with a teenage daughter.

She's chewing with a slice of bacon hanging out of her mouth when she finally decides to share more. "He talked to me once."

Silas sets his glass of juice down hard on the table. I let him continue to take the lead. "When?" he asks through gritted teeth. I glance down and notice one of his hands balled into a fist. *God help the person who threatens Silas Montgomery's baby girl.* Those hands are incredibly strong. I should know. He uses them on me—and not in a bad way.

"The other day while you were at work," she says

nonchalantly. She continues to chew as if this isn't a big deal.

Silas tilts his head down and swallows hard. "What did he say?"

Rosemarie can't swing her leg as easily now that she's in a low chair, but her nervousness makes itself known. "I'm not hungry anymore. My stomach hurts," she says.

I sigh audibly. It's difficult to contain my reaction. "There's no need to be anxious," I say. "We talked about this. Remember? You have to eat, Rosemarie."

My tone is stern. I don't intend for it to be. My intentions don't stop my words from sounding harsh, though. I understand—intellectually—that I should be nicer. Less critical. Slower to react.

Silas shoots me a look. *Stop*, he says with his eyes. He gathers himself, relaxing his fist.

"It's just that I don't want you pulling your hair out anymore," I add. "You'll have a bald spot soon. You don't want to go to school with a bald spot, believe me. That would get you the wrong kind of attention. I know summer break will be here soon, but think about it. They don't even allow hats in the building. You'd have to walk around balding, in plain view, for everyone to see."

My husband closes his eyes and shakes his head slowly. Rosemarie watches us like a little hawk. One that's learning. Soaking it all up so that she, too, can raise a dysfunctional family one day. *Dammit.*

"Meredith, babe," Silas begins, "I left my wallet upstairs in our bedroom. Would you mind grabbing it for me?"

He doesn't offer a reason why he can't go retrieve it

himself—if it's even up there. We all get the picture. I've fucked up again.

I don't mean to. Truly, I don't. Sometimes, it feels like Rosemarie is some alien species that I'll never understand. There should be a manual. They should give it to you at the hospital before you're allowed to take your baby girl home. Who cares that it will be a long while before you'll feel the divergence? The teenage years are such a seismic shift that preparation is absolutely necessary. Critical, I dare say.

"Um hmm," I reply after a pause. I swallow my pride. "I need to grab my makeup bag from the bathroom, anyway. I'll go up and look."

I take a big bite of eggs, then wipe the corners of my mouth with my napkin. I push my chair away from the table and leave the room. Walking softly, I round a corner toward the main staircase, but I don't go any further. I watch and wait, quietly, hoping to overhear the rest of their conversation. I can see them in the reflection of the sliding glass doors to the patio. Alphie stares at me sympathetically, as if he knows my secret. He knows other secrets, too. Secrets that I wish I didn't have to keep. I hope the old dog doesn't give me away.

Silas leans close to our daughter. "You don't have to eat this food if you don't want to," he says. "It's your body. You're in control. You make the rules when it comes to your own body, okay? Always."

She nods, softening. Rosemarie feels seen by her dad. Everyone can tell how close they are.

"I'll tell you, though," he continues, his tone lighter, "I was hoping to stop by Cafe du Monde on the way to school this morning. Best to have something more nutritious in the tank before we eat beignets."

She considers his advice, and quickly concedes. Beignets are a soft spot for Rosemarie. Almost as much as cute dogs. "Okay, Daddy," she says as she lifts her fork and shovels eggs into her mouth. Silas does the same. They eat silently for a while. The sound of silverware clanking against plates fills the room.

Once she's relaxed again, he tries a different approach. "Do you think you could point the man out to me, if I sit with you and watch for him?"

She nods. "Yeah, probably. When are you going to sit and watch with me, though? Won't you have work?"

He shrugs. "The hotels can wait. That's why I have managers who take care of things when I'm not there. I'll just tell them I'm coming in late today." He looks deep into his daughter's eyes. "You're most important to me. You and your mom."

Rosemarie smiles and leans her head on his shoulder. In moments like this, she seems like a little girl. I cherish these times, even when I have to observe from a distance because I'm too dumb to keep my big mouth shut. I don't want our little girl to grow up.

"I know, Daddy," she says. "I didn't tell you about the man because I didn't want you to worry. I don't think he wants to hurt us."

Silas tenses, but works to keep his response measured. "How would you know?"

"I don't. It just doesn't seem like it. I think he's probably a nice man."

"What did he say to you?" Silas asks again, twisting his bottom lip against his thumb.

I watch as Rosemarie tries to kick her leg, then shifts to pulling on a section of hair. I wish she'd quit doing that. I'm afraid it's becoming a real problem.

"I'm not sure I should tell you," she says softly. "I don't want anyone to get in trouble."

Alarm bells go off in my head and I start towards them. I stop by myself after a few steps, though, and I force myself to wait. To let Silas handle it.

"What kind of grown, smoking man talks to fourteen year-old girls when their parents aren't home unless they're up to no good?" I mumble to myself. I glance at Alphie for his agreement. He sticks out his tongue and pants lightly, as if to offer his moral support.

Rosemarie leans over to look in my direction, but she can't see me in the same reflection I'm using to watch her. When I'm quiet again, she turns her attention back to her dad.

Silas narrows his eyes, calculating his response. "Rosemarie, honey, this man could be dangerous," he says. "You need to tell me what he said to you. It doesn't matter what it is or how badly you're scared. You won't be in trouble. You can trust me. I promise."

She scrunches her nose. "It isn't me who will be in trouble," she clarifies.

"Then who?" he asks, confused.

Before she can answer, the doorbell rings and all three dogs begin barking. Alphie leads the charge, woofing in his most protective tone. The pups gather at the front doors and peer through the glass panes that begin at their eye level.

"Hush, dogs," Silas says, his voice a bit rattled.

People who don't know him wouldn't be able to tell, but I can. He's shaken up. He *sees* something that has him shaken up. I can't imagine what, because I'm the one who should be on guard.

Silas doesn't know about the threats I've received in recent weeks. He doesn't know the family history and resulting burden I've been saddled with thanks to my mom's poor decisions. He doesn't know that trouble may have finally come knocking, with my name written all over it.

He tells Rosemarie to stay put, then walks to the foyer to answer the door. He motions for the dogs to stay, too, as he smiles politely and steps outside onto the porch.

3
____

FOUNDATIONS
RUTHIE

Nashville

"Hello, there, old broad!" Mitch says, his tone far too jovial to suit me.

"Mitch Weller," I grumble.

We aren't even that old. Not really. I had Meredith when I was in my early twenties. I was one of the youngest mothers among those in our social circles. If you ask me, I'm too young to be dying of heart failure. But I digress.

I hate it when men like Mitch think they're funnier than they actually are. He's a washed up old coot, truth be told. I'm surprised he isn't on *his* deathbed somewhere. It doesn't seem fair that he's out working, traveling, and wreaking all kinds of havoc while my life comes to an inauspicious end.

"You finally decided to take my call," he mutters smugly.

"To what do I owe the pleasure?" I ask in my best fake-nice voice, even though I'm the one who solicited him. I plaster on a smile to aid the effect. I don't think it's working.

Dahlia rolls her eyes as if to tell me I should behave. She sits back down on the side of my bed, tucking the edges of her skirt underneath her legs again. She's listening closely, hanging on my every word. Sometimes, I think she wants this reunion to happen even more than I do. She has taken up my cause, in earnest.

A noise that sounds like a boat horn blows in the distance on the other end of the phone. "I have news," Mitch says. "The kind you'll definitely want me to share. In fact, Pete would kill me if I kept something like this to myself, God rest his soul."

I stiffen at the mention of my husband. "Come now, Mitch, we don't need to bring Pete into this, do we?"

Dahlia shakes her head and rolls her eyes again—harder this time. She knows most of the backstory. She knows almost all of my stories. "Let the man speak," she whispers.

I shrug.

"I reckon not," Mitch replies. "Good ol' Pete isn't here. It's just me and you, Ruth."

"Ruthie," I say sternly, correcting him. "No one calls me Ruth anymore."

He laughs a hearty laugh, and I can imagine his broad shoulders heaving up and down. He was a trusted confidant once. I'm not so sure he can be again. There is a river of bad blood between us. Pete would be the first to warn me about getting too close.

"How have you been?" I ask, the fake-nice persona still on. I smile again as I say the words. I don't *genuinely* care to hear how the man has been. I want to learn what he knows about my daughter. I have to play coy, though. I shouldn't act too eager. I don't intend to let him know that he has leverage on me. "And was that a boat horn I heard in the background?" I ask. "Sounded like a big one."

"I'm good," he says. "You heard right. It was a boat—probably going under the Causeway Bridge. I'm parked by the water."

"Which body of water?" I ask, quickly thinking of all the causeways I can bring to mind.

I have Mitch investigating my daughter, but I don't yet know where she lives. She has managed to keep her life completely hidden from me. I've tried—hard—to find her on my own. I wouldn't have hired Mitch if there had been any other choice.

I motion for Dahlia, pointing to a pen and notepad on my nightstand. When she hands them to me, I scribble the words causeway and bridge with a question mark. She purses her lips as she thinks. "Florida?" she mouths.

"A body of water that won't be named just yet," Mitch says. "You know the rules."

I can practically hear the satisfaction in his voice. He wants to string me along. "You'd withhold that information from a dying old woman?" I quip. "I don't know how strong I sound over the phone, but I assure you I'm dying very soon. I spent the better part of yesterday writing my own obituary."

"Jesus, Ruth … err, Ruthie," he replies. "That's morbid."

"That's where I'm at in life," I say as I tilt my head to lean the phone receiver on my shoulder. "It's no joke for me. Morbid might as well be my middle name. One foot in the grave and all."

I narrow my eyes as I think harder about causeways and scribble city names to show Dahlia. Miami and Fort Myers come to mind, so I write them down. Dahlia looks at me again as she gets an idea of her own. "Texas?" she mouths this time. She takes the pen and writes Galvaston alongside a question mark.

"I'm sorry to hear that," Mitch says, striking a more serious tone. "All joking aside. I hate what you're going through. I care about you, you know? I always have and I always will."

"Thanks for that," I say. We did care about each other —deeply. Although, that was a long time ago. Surprised by his display of kindness, I turn my full attention back to our conversation. "So, tell me what you found out about Meredith. Please. Tell me where she lives. She's married, right? Is she still married?"

I instantly regret sounding so vulnerable. Yet I *am* vulnerable, in the worst way possible. My days are literally numbered, and I don't want to leave this world without making things right. The need to reconcile with my daughter has become all encompassing. I can hardly think of anything else lately.

This sucks. How did I get here?

He sighs and I hear his breath through the phone. "I know where she lives," he says. "I found her, just like you asked."

"You do?" My heart practically leaps out of my chest at this news. "That's … that's amazing," I say. "Incredible.

Good job, Mitch. Very, very good work. I may grumble, but I knew I could count on you."

It's been nearly fifteen years since I've spoken to my Meredith. Every single day since I last heard her voice has been torture. I wasn't sure I'd ever find her. Although, doing so now is just the beginning. We have miles to go before she'll talk to me, let alone forgive me for what I've done.

It's my dying wish to be forgiven.

"I do," he confirms. "She's still married. To a tall black man who looks a helluva lot like Pete, actually. If you ask me."

I clutch a handful of blanket to steady myself. "Really? He looks like my Pete?"

Dahlia's face lights up. She's excited, too.

"He does," Mitch confirms. "You know what they say about daddy's girls."

"What do they say?" I ask.

He laughs, but not in a mocking way. He's easing up on me. "That they grow up and marry someone much like their daddies, that's all. I guess our girl went and did just that."

"She isn't *our* anything," I snap.

"Yeah, sorry."

I pause, breathing deeply as I decide how to handle this information. Like a kid in a candy store, I want it all, and as irritating as Mitch is, he's giving me an amazing gift. I can't exactly get out of this bed to go find her myself. I need Mitch. Desperately.

Still thinking about causeways, Dahlia waves a hand to get my attention then mouths, "Georgia?" She writes

Brunswick on the pad. It occurs to me that our list could be completed more quickly with the help of Google. I point to her phone, and she nods then begins typing furiously with both thumbs.

"I think Pete would have liked that," I say. "Can you imagine the look on his face?"

Mitch laughs heartily again, cautiously testing the limits of our rapport. "He'd smile so big."

"So big," I agree.

We're silent for a moment as Dahlia Googles. My heart randomly feels like it skips a beat, reminding me of its failings.

Your time is running out.

I feel that more than ever.

Finding something online, Dahlia sits up straight and grabs for the pad and pen. She looks like she has the answer. She quickly scribbles New Orleans and circles it several times for emphasis.

"New Orleans?" I ask out loud. "Lake Pontchartrain?" I add as Dahlia writes the body of water. She nods approvingly, satisfied that we've made such short work out of the task. Mitch stays silent on the other end of the phone, letting me know we've guessed right. "That's it, isn't it? Meredith went to New Orleans on a school trip in the seventh grade. She always talked about how much she liked the place. Plus, it isn't so different from Nashville. Both cities have that southern charm everyone raves about. I should have known."

Dahlia nods. "Good work, partner," she says as she raises a gentle hand to give me high five. "Southern charm for the win."

"I didn't confirm anything," Mitch says feebly.

He clears his throat gruffly, and I recognize his old nervous habit. "You didn't have to," I reply.

The tension is suddenly so thick, you could cut it with a knife. It's a strange dance that we're doing, Mitch and I. Up and down. Rigid, then relaxed. It almost feels like the steps have been choreographed in advance, perhaps by some invisible hand guiding my fate. Pete's?

"What are you thinking about?" Mitch asks when I'm quiet for too long. It's a bold, intimate question.

"Everything," I say, "and nothing. Well, to be honest, I'm thinking about Pete, mostly."

Sensing that I could use a little privacy, Dahlia excuses herself to take care of the laundry. My worsening incontinence means the poor dear washes a minimum of three to four loads each day. "Be back in a jiffy," she whispers on her way out. I smile my thanks, then lean my head against the pillow and close my eyes.

"Mitch?" I ask.

"Yeah, Ruth?"

I let his infraction slide. He called me Ruth for years. I understand that old habits are hard to break.

"Do you think she's happy? In New Orleans, with her nice husband who looks a lot like Pete? Do they seem … content?"

Every mother wants her child to be happy. At the end of the day and at the heart of it all, it's what we want for them. Simply for them to be happy. It's an elusive, tangential concept, yet we crave checking that box. As if we'll know our job is done and it's okay to rest when the kid has grown up and is *happy*. As I can attest, that's true even when we've given them plenty of reasons to be unhappy. In my case, even when we've given them one huge, monumental reason to be unhappy.

"I don't know," he says softly. "It's hard to tell. I've only been watching for a short time. I can't get too close, or they'll notice me and call the cops. I mostly park by the lake and track down leads on my laptop while keeping one eye on their house."

"By Lake Pontchartrain," I say. "New Orleans."

"That's right," he concedes after a beat. "They seem like a happy family."

A jolt moves through me like a bolt of lightning. My heart thumps and I become short of breath. I want to ask, though. I want to *know*. "Why did you say *family*?"

He grunts and I can imagine him shrugging. "It's a word people use."

"Sure, but why did you say family instead of couple?" I press. "If it's just Meredith and her husband, wouldn't you have called them a couple?"

"Silas," Mitch adds.

"What?"

"Her husband's name is Silas. By all accounts, he's a good man. He owns a chain of popular boutique hotels in the New Orleans area. His reputation is that of an honest businessperson and a generous employer. No one I've talked to has had a negative word to say about him."

I'm taken aback, pleased with this information about my son-in-law, but I don't want to remove my focus from the prize. "Okay," I say. "So, if it's just Meredith and Silas there, why didn't you call them a couple?" I take a deep breath and shift in bed, waiting. "Well?" I ask, growing exasperated.

Mitch stammers. He's holding back. Why?

"I can tell you more about Meredith if you like," he offers. "Get this—she's an interior designer, just like you."

My jaw drops. "Are you serious?"

"Serious as a heart attack—" he says, then stops himself. "Shit. I'm sorry."

I shrug it off. "Just something people say," I reply, my ailing heart seeming to twitch inside my chest at the irony of it all.

"Right.," he says. "Yeah, she's part owner in a high-end firm with another woman. They're based in the area north of the lake known as the North Shore. It's full of well-to-do types, and it seems like business is good. Meredith is even in the middle of a multimillion-dollar renovation on her already stunning home."

"Wow," I say. "I don't think I could have guessed that she'd follow in my footsteps. I mean, she grew up traipsing around furniture stores and makers' markets with me. She certainly had the right background for a career in interior design. I suppose I expected her to do something totally different, though, just so she wasn't too much like me. You know?"

"Understood," Mitch says. "I guess the apple didn't fall far from the tree. Be glad she's followed in your footsteps. I'm no expert in such matters, but her style strikes me as a lot like yours."

"How so?" I probe, fascinated.

My mind puts together a scene where my daughter is all grown up, dressed fashionably and consulting with clients at a posh, impeccably decorated office. It isn't about status for me. I genuinely love design. Colors, textures, and materials have always given me a thrill. I've spent my career working with rich clients simply because they can afford to hire me. Poor folks, sadly, don't have the luxury of spending money on a decorator. I assume my daughter found out the same, and apparently, she has the personal wealth to show for it. I want her to experience all the best our chosen career field has to offer.

"You know I can't describe that sort of thing," Mitch says. "Her office and her house both look real nice. In fact, her home on the lake reminds me of your place in Brentwood. You are still living there, right? Up on the hill?"

"I am," I say, most interested in talking about Meredith, not about myself. "Tell me about her house."

It sounds like he smiles, because his voice lightens. "It's big," he says with a chuckle. "She's done well for herself. The place must be five-thousand square feet or more."

"What color?"

"White, like yours," he replies. "I told you. The whole place looks a lot like yours. Gray shutters."

I smile now, too. "What shade of gray?"

"Seriously?"

"Humor me," I say, feeling easy and free for the moment. It feels like old times. "Like a silver gray? Or more of a pewter?"

"Ruth," he says, the name becoming a comfortable habit again, "I couldn't tell silver from pewter if my life depended on it. You know that. What do you think I am? I must stay in my lane, woman."

"Fine," I say. "Silver or charcoal? You can tell the difference between silver and charcoal, can't you?"

He laughs some more. "Fine. The shutters are more silver than charcoal. There. Are you happy?"

"In that regard, for now … yes," I confirm. "I am happy. Thank you. What does the front of the house look like? Is there a porch?"

"Oh, yeah, a big one that stretches all the way across the front," he explains. "It has ceiling fans that turn around and around on hot days like today. The whole place is raised up high, so floodwaters don't ruin the inside if a tropical storm rolls through. That means there are steps stretching up to the porch. Let's see. I'll count them. One, two, three … looks like fifteen or sixteen steps to …"

"Wait a minute," I say, interrupting. "You're there now? At Meredith's house?"

He hesitates. "Um, yeah. I told you, I park by the lake and keep an eye on the place. Why?"

My heart beats faster. "I didn't realize you were right there. So close. You could knock on the door. You could talk to my daughter. Tell her I'm trying to reach her. You could even hand the phone to her and let me talk." My voice becomes frantic.

I grab hold of my blanket again and try to remain calm. I could hasten my own demise if I push my ailing heart too far. I have to pace myself. To stay alive long enough.

"Whoa, whoa, whoa," Mitch says. "You're forgetting an important piece of information."

"Yeah?" I ask. "What's that?'

"Meredith would probably recognize me, if she saw

me up close. I can't just waltz up there and talk to her like a friendly neighborhood paperboy or anything."

"She was a kid the last time she saw you. At Pete's funeral, right?" I ask, driving home the fact that Mitch disappeared from our lives when Pete died. It's a fact that isn't lost on him. "That was twenty years ago. Who says she'll even remember your name."

"Come on, now," he says. "There's no reason to be mean. Meredith grew up thinking of me as an honorary uncle. Of course, she'll remember my name. She'll remember *me*. Plus, she was twenty-two when Pete died. Hardly a kid. You're reaching, Ruth."

I feel desperate. I want to get to her so badly. Thanks to this conversation, I have a lot of new information that Dahlia and I can search for on the internet. But Mitch is right. I have to be reasonable. To take this slow. My daughter went to a good deal of effort to keep me from finding her all these years. If I move too quickly or push too hard, she'll never be open to a reconciliation.

Perhaps I'll need to think outside of the box. My smart mind and imagination are the best weapons I've got at this juncture. If I can't get to Meredith the usual way, perhaps I can find another path to her inner world. Come to think of it, I might be able to use her renovation project to my advantage. After all, who better to be the eyes and ears inside a home than the designers hired to make renovations? I like that idea. It's unusual, but it has potential. I decide to let it percolate.

"Okay, okay," I say. "I miss her, Mitch. So sue me for being overeager. I don't exactly have a lot of time. They've told me my life expectancy is weeks to months. Whatever that means."

"I get it," he says solemnly. "This is important—to the both of us. Let me keep watching. Keep investigating. I'll figure out the best way to approach her. I'll do it as fast as possible. I promise. We're walking a fine line."

"So, that's it?" I ask. "I just have to sit here on my deathbed and wait?"

His voice warms and he lets out a soft moan that sounds like grief. "I'm sorry, Ruth. I truly am. From the bottom of my heart. I never thought it would end this way. With you in this … tight spot. You deserve better."

He pauses before continuing, and I realize I'm no longer angry with him. He's not so bad. What happened back then wasn't his fault. In fact, maybe I projected my pain onto Mitch. Maybe it was easier to hate him than myself. The revelation is a pleasant surprise. I should have reached out to him sooner.

"Thank you," I say simply, unable to put my feelings into words quickly enough to share them with him.

As I pause, collecting my thoughts, I can only hope Mitch intuits the shape of my silence. I need him on my side. I need him in what's left of my life.

"Hey," he says, finally, "how about I send you a picture of Meredith's house to tide you over until we speak again? I'll even try to get one from the side street so you can see the massive pool out back."

"There's a pool? Does it have fountains? Can you tell if it's saltwater?" I ask, my voice rising.

Now we're talking. I smile as I imagine the property.

"I think it has a fountain, yeah," Mitch says. I can hear

gulls squawking in the distance, their voices insistent. "I'll get a picture. But don't ask me to name the specific color of the water, because I'll tell you it's swimming pool blue." He laughs, then I do, too.

"Text me the pictures, okay?" I ask. "Email them also, to be sure I get them. You have my mobile number and my email address?"

"I do," Mitch confirms. It's quiet on the line for a moment, then he circles back to the reason he called in the first place. "Do you want to know the thing that Pete would kill me if I didn't share?"

"Well, well, well. Aren't you bold, talking about Pete killing *you*?" I ask. "Ain't that some shit?"

I'm feeling bolder. Less burdened by our history and more buoyed by it. Perhaps it's okay to joke around a bit. Doing so might even be fun.

"Ruth," he says, ignoring my jab, "do you want to know, or what?"

I sit up straight in bed. I suppose I'm deflecting. I didn't think he was going to say anything more about my family during this conversation. I'm bolstered by the possibilities of what I'm about to hear. "Yes!" I exclaim. "Of course. Forgive me. Tell me what you know, Mitch! Please."

He takes a long, deep breath, then says words that are the most beautiful music to my ears. Words that until today, I hadn't expected to hear. Not in my wildest dreams.

"Ruth, honey," Mitch says, "you have a granddaughter. Her name is Rosemarie and she's fourteen years-old. She has your dazzling smile."

4

SHE NEEDED ME
MEREDITH

New Orleans

I can't see the person who rang the bell. "Who is it?" I call, causing Rosemarie to whip her head around in my direction.

"Mom?"

Damn, I think. Now she'll probably know I've been listening to their conversation this whole time.

"Yep," I say as I rejoin her at the table. "Right here."

"Did you find Daddy's wallet?" she asks.

I'm distracted by whoever is at the door and am debating whether to step out onto the porch. "What?" I ask her.

"Daddy's wallet," she says again.

"Oh, yes," I reply, remembering what I'd been tasked with. "Right. I was headed upstairs to look."

"Did you find it?"

I lower my brow, trying hard to hear what's happening

out there. "No, I didn't," I say. "He must have left it somewhere else. We'll find it."

I don't share that I never went to the second level of our home. This isn't the time. Rosemarie shrugs, not terribly concerned.

"Hey, who is at the door?" I ask, as casually as I can. "Did Dad say?"

Rosemarie shakes her head, not seeming to associate the concern about the strange man watching us and someone ringing our doorbell this early in the morning. Little does she know just how dangerous this unexpected visitor could be. "Nope," she replies. "But Dad said we can swing by Cafe du Monde for beignets on the way to school. Can you come with us?"

Her brown eyes shine and she looks genuinely excited, like she wants me to go. I relish this small victory. She wants me. Not just her dad, but me too. I return her smile.

"I think I can do that," I say. "Let me text Becca so she knows I'll be a little late today. We have a meeting with a new client at eleven and I had planned to prep beforehand, but I'm fairly certain she can handle it on her own."

My daughter looks at me, wary of my excuses and with little interest in the details. I take note. It's better if I keep work talk brief when I'm around Rosemarie. I suppose that's fair. I felt the same way about my mom.

"So, you can go?" she asks.

"I can," I confirm. "Cafe du Monde it is! It'll be nice to spend some special time together. Beignets are always a treat."

She jumps up and down with child-like enthusiasm, then she hugs me. She *really* hugs me. Tightly. I close my eyes and soak it in. I don't want my girl and me to grow apart. I want to do better than my mom did. I want to break the cycle. To fix what went wrong. Rosemarie didn't ask to be born to a parent with emotional baggage. She deserves my best efforts to do better.

Suddenly, a loud whack rings out from somewhere outside. It sounds like it came from the front of the house. I can't tell what made the sound. A slamming door maybe? A belt being snapped? That doesn't make any sense. My mind struggles to place what I heard.

"Silas?" I call. "Is everything okay?" I scramble to get to him. Something isn't right. I can feel it. "Silas?"

The dogs whine and pace restlessly, staring up at me for reassurance. Rosemarie reaches for Alphie, who has moved to her side. "Mommy," she says as she wraps an arm around his strong neck, "I'm scared."

Her choice to call me Mommy sinks deep. I feel loved and accepted. My little girl still needs me, after all. But I don't want to stoke the fires of unnecessary drama to gain her acceptance. I tell myself to remain calm.

Hopefully, this is nothing to worry about. Maybe a paperboy, signing up subscribers for his new route. Or the utility company, informing us about a service interruption due to necessary maintenance. Those things are within the realm of possibility, right?

"It's okay," I say, buoyed by Rosemarie's faith in me. "There's no need to be scared. You stay here. I'm going out with Daddy ... to see what that sound was."

She nods, then peers out one of the windows

overlooking the front yard. When the scene comes into view, the pink drains from her cheeks and her muscles go as stiff as a board.

"What is it?" I ask. "What do you see?"

This is escalating too quickly. I must slow things down. I must project confidence. I must be reasonable.

Tears form in the corners of Rosemarie's eyes. "The silver car that belongs to the smoking man," she mutters, pointing. "That's it. Right there, across the street." She leaps back toward me, wrapping her arms around my waist. "I'm scared he'll hurt Daddy."

I open my mouth to reassure her, but I honestly have no idea what this is all about so I close my mouth again.

The smoking man might be related to the threats I've received, or he might not. The people who have contacted me seem aggressive, whereas this smoking guy has, apparently, been hanging out for days without bothering anything. As far as we know.

I think about what to say to Rosemarie. Do I really believe that everything will be okay? My gut tells me I shouldn't lie to my daughter. Yet what is the truth? What's the proper tone to strike? It feels like walking a tightrope. Not that it's so different from any other day since she has become a teenager.

"It's too early for this," I mutter, glancing at the clock on the wall. I'm not much of a morning person.

"Mommy?" Rosemarie asks again as Alphie wedges himself between us. He follows her gaze through the window. It's just out of my line of sight.

"Your daddy is a big, strong man," I say, unsure what

else to offer. "He is very capable of taking care of himself."

"And us?"

I nod. That, I can confirm. "And us." Of course, even a big, strong, capable man has his limits. I don't mention those.

"He *is* big and strong," Rosemarie says with a slight smile.

"Besides," I continue, "didn't you say that you don't think the smoking man would hurt us?" Realizing my mistake, my face falls. I've done it again. Insert foot into mouth.

"You were listening," she says warily. "Of course, you were listening. Spying is more like it. You should get a life."

"Not on purpose," I lie, then I think better of it. "Well, maybe it was sort of on purpose, but not to be rude or disrespectful. I care about you. I want to be sure you're okay. One day, when you have a daughter of your own, you might understand."

Rosemarie looks up at me and stares into my eyes as if she can read into the depths of my very soul. I feel so exposed with this child. I'm not sure how to handle it. "Did your mom say that to you when you were my age?"

I cringe. "You know I don't like talking about my childhood—or my mom."

"She's my grandma," Rosemarie says, still holding onto me. She takes the chance to press the subject. "I have a right to know about my own grandma. Is she dead?"

I furrow my brow. "How did we get on this subject?

We were talking about a noise on the porch and the person who knocked."

"What's her name then?" she asks. "If you won't tell me anything else about her, at least tell me her name."

I've purposely kept that information to myself. No one in my current life except Silas knows my mother's name. In this day and age, she could be found with a few strokes of the keyboard. That's the last thing I want. The very last thing.

Rosemarie senses my distress. "Mom, you're being ridiculous again. What could Grandma possibly have done that's so bad? It's not fair that you won't even tell me her name."

"I … I have my reasons," I stammer. "You are too young to understand." It irks me the way she calls her Grandma, as if the woman is a friendly storybook character knitting mittens and baking cookies. Not that we need mittens down here, anyway.

"I'll be eighteen one day, and then I'll do whatever I want," my daughter declares rebelliously. "You can't control me forever."

Wow. That hurts.

"You think so," I say, my voice breaking, "but hopefully, you will mature between now and then. I pray you'll come to see the wisdom in my ways. If I hadn't kept you away from her, who knows what our lives would be like? She's toxic. And that's putting it mildly. Your dad understands. Ask him if you don't believe me."

"Sounds like a tired old excuse," she says curtly.

She isn't wrong, but it's complicated.

Before we can argue the point any further, a gust of

wind comes along and causes the American Flag hung out front to flap against its mount. The porch swing follows suit, creaking as it's carried in the breeze. We both jump.

"Where is your dad?" I ask, keen to change the subject and legitimately wondering what's going on with my husband.

Rosemarie tightens her hold on my waist, and I'm stuck by how swiftly her emotions seem to vacillate. She can go from warm and cuddly to icy cold—and back—in the blink of an eye. Was I like that when I was a teenager?

"I don't know," she says. Her voice is genial, and her face has softened again. "I wish we could see him. I don't like this. I want to know, for sure, that he's okay."

"Me too."

Alphie glances up at us, then at the other dogs. He's in charge. He's waiting to see how we intend to handle this so he can tell the others.

After a moment of silence while we wait, Rosemarie blurts. "The smoking man asked me about you," she says quickly. "I was sitting in one of the Adirondack chairs down by the firepit the other day. He came up to the fence and asked if Meredith Flores lived here, but he didn't say Montgomery. Why didn't he say Meredith Flores Montgomery?"

"Rosemarie!" I exclaim, unable to hide the worry on my face. "Why didn't you say anything to us about this before now? *Why* were you outside alone? Do you *know* what happens to kids who talk to strangers?"

"What's the big deal?" she asks. "I was inside our fence. People walking by stop and talk to me all the time. They like our dogs."

"All the time?" I ask. "You should be inside the house when we aren't home. You aren't allowed to be in the yard. Do you know how dangerous—?"

"Yeah, yeah," she says as she pulls away from me and rolls her eyes. "I'm your prisoner. I have to stay inside all alone while you and Daddy work day and night. The only time I'm allowed to leave my cage is when I go to school. I get it. I'll soon be your captive for the summer. Can't wait." Her tone is dripping with animosity.

"Huh," I scoff. "That's what you think? I really do hope you mature by the time you turn eighteen. You will have a rude awakening when you get out into the real world if you don't."

"Whatever."

I take a breath. No matter how unpleasant this conversation is, I have to learn more about what my daughter knows. I need to find out if this man is connected to the people who contacted me. I must determine how serious the threat actually is. I've wondered if they're blowing smoke.

"What did he say to you?" I ask.

"I told you," she replies. "He asked if Meredith Flores lives here. That was your name before you married Daddy and added Montgomery on the end, right?"

I nod. "Yes, that's right. How did you respond to him?"

She pauses, and she seems afraid to tell me the truth. One thing my daughter is not, however, is a liar. She gets that from her dad. She might omit information or delay telling us, but she won't speak anything that's untrue. She follows a strict moral code.

"It's okay. You said yes. You told him that I live here. I get it," I say.

"Don't be mad, Mom," she grumbles. "I didn't think about your weird issues with your mom when I was talking to the man. He asked a simple question, and I answered. He could have looked at the mail in our mailbox and found out what he wanted to know."

"Tampering with mail is a federal offense," I say.

"Yeah, and opening a mailbox to look at the name on an envelope isn't a big deal. Get a grip. Besides, he could have found you on the internet."

I shake my head. "Not necessarily. I'm very careful to keep my name off the internet. I like my privacy."

"You like hiding from Grandma. She could find you if she wanted to."

I open my mouth to counter Rosemarie's accusation, but she's right. I stop myself and reconsider my approach. Instead of arguing, I smile my most genuine smile and reach my arms out to embrace her. Someone has to be the hero in our relationship. That someone almost certainly needs to be me.

She leans her head against me and I smooth her hair. "It's time for me to go outside and find out what's happening. Okay?" I cradle her cheeks in my hands and look hard into her eyes.

"Okay," she confirms as another loud whack sounds from somewhere out front. We both jump again and the dogs start a new round of protective woofs. Alphie leads the charge.

"You stay here with the dogs," I say. "Keep your phone on you—just in case. You have it, right?"

She reaches into a pocket then holds it up to show me. "Yes, Mommy. It's right here."

I'm Mommy again. I know it will be fleeting, but I relish it.

"I don't think you'll need to, but call 9-1-1 if—"

"If what?" she asks, her dark eyes wide with worry.

I reconsider. "You know, dear daughter, don't worry about that yet. We're getting ahead of ourselves. Stay here. It will be fine," I say.

I don't want to alarm my child. I spent what felt like my entire childhood on high alert, always nervous, always walking on eggshells. That was so I didn't set my mom off. This is different. *Mostly. Maybe. I don't know.* Once childhood memories are involved, things get terribly tangled in my mind. I pause, collecting myself, and I focus my attention on Rosemarie.

"Go ahead," she says.

She nods, but her breathing is shallow. It makes me wonder if there's more to the story about the smoking man and what he said to her. No time to find out just yet. I want to lay eyes on my husband and be sure he isn't in trouble. There will be time to chat over beignets.

I move to hug Rosemarie once more. As I do, we hear a much bigger thump. It's so loud, it rattles the decorative plates hung on a wall near the windows. Rosemarie lets out a scream. She quickly covers her mouth, stopping the sound.

"What the fuck?" I ask.

Rosemarie is too preoccupied to scold me for my bad language.

Sara takes the lead, woofing furiously, then Alphie and

Calliope provide backup. All three dogs join us near the front door. They surround us, although I'm not sure whether they intend to defend us or they are scared and want us to safeguard them.

This is getting more and more concerning by the minute. Have I underestimated the threats I've received? For my family's sake, I sincerely hope not.

My phone buzzes from its position on the kitchen counter. I narrow my eyes, working to process all that's happening. "Who could that be?" I ask.

Rosemarie doesn't skip a beat. She realizes what it is before I do. "It's an alert, not a call," she says. "From the doorbell camera."

"Oh, right," I say. "I should get my phone and take a look."

An eerie silence settles over us as everything goes still. I'm not sure whether we should be afraid. For all I know, Silas will walk back in the front door any minute with a perfectly reasonable explanation for the sounds we've heard. On the other hand, what if he doesn't? The longer he's out there, the more uneasy I'm becoming. Something strange is happening, for sure.

"He'll see you," Rosemarie says.

"What?"

"If you get your phone, you'll walk past those other windows and he'll be able to see you," she explains.

"Who are you talking about?" I ask.

"The smoking man," she replies. "If he's in his car, he'll see you."

A surge of adrenaline gives me strength as something shifts inside me. I've had enough. I refuse to cower in my own home just because we heard some noises and a man has asked Rosemarie about me. Sure, trouble might find us. I've known that since the day I cut ties with my mother and moved south to Louisiana. I won't cower, though. Not today. Not *any* day, if I can help it.

"You know what?" I ask. "Let him see me. Your dad wasn't too scared to step outside, and I'm not either. Whatever is going on, we'll handle it. We're the adults here. We will keep you safe. I promise."

My daughter nods. "Okay." She seems to like my display of confidence.

I guide Rosemarie to a spot away from the windows and give her a reassuring glance. "I'll be back," I say as I grab my phone, motion for the dogs to stay, and step out onto the front porch. I close the door tightly behind me, then survey the scene. I don't see Silas. I don't see anyone, actually. It's eerily quiet, except for the mewing of some gulls cruising over the lake. "Silas?" I call. "Are you out here?"

I crane my neck and look toward the driveway on the side of the house. I can see the back of my husband's red Land Rover. He's still here.

"Mommy!" Rosemarie calls through the windows. "Be careful!"

I wave her back, then open my phone to take a look at the alerts from the doorbell camera. "There has to be something useful here," I mutter. I keep an eye out for any movement around the house as I peer at the small screen in my hands.

A series of recorded clips are in the app's library. The first shows Silas stepping outside. I can see his back and shoulders, but the person he's talking to is positioned on the side, out of frame. I didn't think that was even possible. The camera is supposed to cover the entire porch and front yard. I quickly flip through the other clips. They're the same—Silas' back as he's talking to someone just out of frame. Until the last one, when my husband can be seen leaving the porch and heading toward the driveway.

"What are you doing?" I ask out loud. "Who are you following?"

I glance inside the house to make sure Rosemary is staying put, then I walk to the driveway, following my husband's path. The wind blows hard again, a gust nearly knocking toppling a small potted plant on the table as I pass by. Even though the breeze is warm, it sends a shiver down my spine. I'm out of sorts. Something disturbing is going on.

As I walk, I eye the silver car parked on the road that Rosemarie insists belongs to the smoking man. I can't tell for sure if anyone is inside. The low morning light casts shadows that prevent me from getting a good view. If he's the person Silas is talking to, I'm not sure how I feel about it. I have a million questions for that man, namely, I'd like to know why he's approaching our daughter when her parents aren't home. I don't care who sent him or what he's trying to accomplish. That's not cool.

Suddenly, my musing is interrupted by the sound of a door slamming on the side of the house.

"Hey! Get out of there!" I hear Silas shout.

A few seconds later, a man—presumably Rosemarie's smoking man—bursts out of the silver car and sprints at full speed up our driveway. The gate only slows him down for a moment as he unfastens the hinge and makes his way inside.

"This is private property!" I yell, the words coming out slurred. There's a lag between my brain and my mouth as I work to process what's happening.

The man continues running, ignoring my warning. I hear banging on a door around the side, then glass breaking.

"Rosemarie!" Silas shouts. "Hide! Get in a bedroom, then lock and barricade the door!"

"What?" I gasp as I quicken my pace. "Silas, what are you talking about?"

The smoking man reaches my husband just as I round the corner and the scene comes into full view. "I'm here to help," the man says, winded but determined. He's older, with graying hair and a bit of a belly.

Silas looks at him, confused, but doesn't have time to ask many questions. "Who?" he manages.

Rosemarie shrieks inside the house, her voice filled with terror. The sound makes my blood run cold. That's my baby in there. My whole world.

"Let's get to him, before he hurts your daughter," the man insists. "There will be time to hash things out later."

I interject. "How do we know you aren't *with* him? Why should we trust you?" My voice is strained. It doesn't sound quite right coming out.

The man turns to face me and for the first time, I can see his features plainly. I gasp. I know this man. It's been a long, long time, but I'd know him anywhere.

When he sees the recognition on my face, he nods

sheepishly then turns back to Silas. "I'm a friend of her parents," he says. That's debatable, but he definitely knew my parents. I grew up thinking of him as an honorary uncle.

Shaken but resigned, I gesture for Silas to accept Mitch Weller's help, and to let him in.

5

A WORLD AWAY

RUTHIE

Nashville

Less is more. That's what they always say. I hope the advice holds true for packing a suitcase because I'll be traveling light. I used to love having fabulous outfits and accessories for every occasion. It's now imperative that I save my strength for more important tasks. Fabulous outfits won't help me where I'm going.

I'm wrestling with luggage in the back of my closet—oxygen tank in tow—when Dahlia finds me.

"Helen Ruth Flores!" she practically shouts. "What are you doing, pray tell? You had better get back in bed right this minute."

Her words send a jolt through me. I turn in her direction and narrow my eyes. "Don't boss me around, young lady. I didn't tell you my full name for you to use it against me," I say.

She makes a clicking noise and shakes her head. "Sorry. I didn't mean any disrespect. It's just—"

"Just nothing," I say. "I'm going to New Orleans." Dahlia remains silent, probably trying to decide how to handle me. "To meet my granddaughter," I add. It's a bold statement. I know that.

Her eyes widen. "I see," she says softly. She's made a quick recovery from her earlier outburst, but she doesn't react to mention of me having a granddaughter. Not like she would if the revelation was a surprise.

"You knew?" I ask.

"Mitch hinted," she replies. "So, yeah, I guess I knew. But it wasn't my place to discuss. I didn't ask questions."

I sigh. I'm frustrated with Dahlia for being harsh with me. At the same time, though, I'm over the moon at the revelation about my granddaughter and I want to share. Enthusiasm wins out. "It's pretty amazing news, don't you think?" I ask.

I probably sound like a child, all hopeful and optimistic. I'm probably kidding myself. There will be complications. Certainly, there will be complications. My plan is becoming firmer in my mind, though. I've already made contact with a colleague in Louisiana to get the ball rolling.

Dahlia leans on the doorframe leading to my ample closet and appraises me from a handful of feet away. At least, she hasn't rushed to try to physically move me yet. "Of course, Ruthie," she coos. "I'm so happy for you. That's why I wanted so badly for you to take Mitch's calls. You could have known a few days earlier if you hadn't been stubborn. You could stand to work on that."

"I'm glad you encouraged me to talk to him," I say. "You were right, as usual. That old coot has given me the most meaningful gift I could ever receive. In the knick of time. That's why I'm going to New Orleans. I have to meet her. I don't care if it kills me—"

We both bristle at the phrasing. We know that it literally could … kill me.

I shake my head, then turn back to the task at hand. The plastic tubing that connects the oxygen tank to the cannula in my nose strains under the pressure as I reach for a neck pillow where it sits high on a shelf. I use all of my energy to stretch tall. I nearly topple over, but at the last second, I clasp my hand around the pillow and bring it down. A small victory.

"You got it?" Dahlia asks.

I nod. Tension fills the silence, and I suddenly realize I might not be able to make the trip. Dahlia knows that much. I want to try, though. I've got to try. It's my *grandchild*, after all. My only grandchild in this world, and here I am—a world away. I must find a means to bridge the distance. To lay eyes on her. To hug her. To hold her hand. Maybe it isn't too late to leave a good impression. If Meredith won't see me, maybe Rosemary will.

"I'll need to arrange for a driver," I begin, matter-of-factly. "I aim to leave tomorrow morning. I figure it will take me all day today to pack and make travel arrangements." I look at her to see if she'll try to stop me. She peers into my eyes, her gaze fixed. She doesn't move to interfere. I turn my attention back to what I'm doing and I continue. "I'll have to stop frequently to change positions and move around. I should probably break the drive into two days. I'd fly, but getting through BNA would be a nightmare in my current condition. Besides, there's too much I want to take with me. I want to bring things to … *pass down* … to my granddaughter."

Dahlia's shoulders slump, as if she's just been defeated. She can tell how much this means to me. How much it would mean to any old, dying woman who just found out that her genes have been passed down. That a piece of her will live on for longer than she previously thought. That there might be an ounce of grace left for her yet.

"Ruthie," she begins, shaking her head, "it's a lot. You haven't left the house in weeks. You've been weak and you've felt too badly to even go to lunch at Hattie B's— your favorite. If hot chicken can't rouse you, I'm not sure you should be tackling such a risky venture as a trip out of state."

I wave my hand in the air, poo-pooing her concerns. "It's the Nashville traffic that's kept me away from the chicken. Melrose is the closest location, and you know how hard it is to find parking in that area, what with all the new construction and high rises going up. If they had a Hattie's B's here in Brentwood—or even in nearby Franklin—it would be a different story."

I don't mention the fact that I can't drive myself anymore. We both know the unfortunate truth. I'll never drive again. The reality of my physical limitations hangs in the air, as heavy as impending storm clouds on a hot summer day.

"Respectfully, I think it's more than that," Dahlia replies. "You've been so weak, my dear. I don't say that to insult you. It's the fact of your situation."

"Would it make you happy if I eat chicken?" I ask. "We could go to Hattie B's for lunch today."

She shakes her head, almost involuntarily. Her body is saying what she means even when her mouth isn't doing the talking. "I don't think that's a good idea, Ruthie. I could call Rae to bring takeout, but going all the way to Melrose and eating inside would wear you slap out."

"Why not?" I press. "I could use the time to start a packing list. I'll bring my notepad and pen to make notes at the table. If you don't mind, maybe you can help me think of things to take for Rosemarie?"

Dahlia's face lights up. "What a beautiful name," she muses with a broad smile. "Rosemarie." It sounds nice to hear her say it.

"I think so, too," I reply. "Please, Dahlia, listen to me. This is very important. I want you to help me get some things to Rosemarie. Special things of mine that she can remember me by. Things that she might appreciate—if not now, when she's older."

She nods, but she's distracted. I get the vague sense that she notices something about my body. Is there something on my shirt, maybe? I look down, but don't see anything.

"Ruthie?" she asks, taking a step toward me.

"I've been thinking about my mother's jewelry. She had some of the most distinctive pieces, including opals, emeralds, and rubies. She was a bit of an eccentric woman, especially for her day and time. Not one to limit herself to run-of-the-mill jewelry like pearls and diamonds, she collected unusual items such as—"

"Ruthie!" Dahlia exclaims, more insistently. "You're

leaning really far to the right. You seem unsteady. Let's sit you down."

I scoff. I don't feel unsteady. At least, not any more than usual. The hospice nurses have explained ad nauseam about how I can expect a recurring cycle of dramatic decline followed by a period of recovery. I'll admit, I'm not sure where we are in that cycle. I resent the damn cycle, now more than ever. "I'm okay," I say. "I need to get my suitcase onto the bed. So I can begin packing."

"I'm not so sure you're okay," Dahlia says. She pulls out her mobile phone and types furiously, eyeing me as she scrolls through what I can only assume are search results. She must be Googling.

"Why?" I ask. "I'm trying to get things out for Rosemarie, and I wanted to tell you about it. There are some jewels of my mother's that I'd like to give her. They're set in other pieces now, but I thought maybe she could have a few of the stones made into one special ring. One that she helps design."

"Ruthie, look at me," she barks, ignoring my inquiry. Reluctantly, I do as she asks. "Your right arm—is it numb?"

"I don't think so," I say. I glance down and see that my right arm is hanging limp at my side. I'm not alarmed, though. My body has betrayed me before. I fully expect it to do so again. As long as I can hang on long enough to do what I want to for my daughter and granddaughter, I don't suppose it matters how banged up I am when I take my last breath. I don't necessarily need my right arm to be functional. Do I?

"Is it weak?" Dahlia asks, clearly reading a checklist.

I lift the arm lazily. "It's weak all right, but I don't guess it's any weaker than usual."

She purses her lips and scrolls some more. "Can you see out of both eyes? Does your head hurt?"

At this, I chuckle. "I can see," I say. "I can hear, smell, taste, and touch, too. For the record."

Before Dahlia arrived in the doorway, I had been looking around at some of my most special belongings and thinking how I wished I could take them with me when I die. I had opened up the old paper box and traced my fingers along the edge of my wedding veil, still folded neatly all these years after marrying Pete. I had sifted through the jewelry he'd given me, along with a brooch that once belonged to my mother. I'd buried my nose in the collar of Pete's leather jacket while memories of him holding me close against his chest came flooding back. My senses are intact. My situation, however, is incredibly unfair.

"Are you sure you're okay, Ruthie?" she asks. "You aren't looking so good. Your balance seems to be off. Does your head hurt?" She's repeating herself now, forcing the issue.

I wave a hand again, dismissing Dahlia's concern. "My head doesn't hurt any more than usual. My balance is fine—" As the words leave my mouth, my right leg fails me. It suddenly seems controlled by another source entirely. It slides somewhere to the side and I slide down along with it. Within seconds, I find myself in a heap on the floor, the creaky hardwood feeling much harder than I remember. "Ouch," I mutter.

"Oh, no!" Dahlia blurts, unable to keep her composure. "I need to call 9-1-1."

"Don't." I say softly.

She pauses, apparently remembering my wishes. I do not want to spend my final days in a hospital being poked and prodded while doctors prolong the inevitable. "Right," she replies. "Then I should call the hospice nurse. I'll dial her now."

"Anne Li doesn't need to be bothered with this," I say. "Today is her son's birthday, remember? She's off for a couple of days. Leave her be." I wince. Something hurts. I try not to let Dahlia know I'm in pain. I wonder how I'm going to get up. My legs seem to be tangled underneath me like a pretzel.

"Oh, Ruthie," Dahlia mutters, chewing her lip. "You have me worried. I need to call *someone*."

I shrug, doing my best to remain cool, calm, and collected. "Help me up?" I ask.

"In a minute," she says. "I first need to be sure you aren't having a stroke."

"Seriously?" I ask. "Does whatever you're reading tell you to leave the person who might be having a stroke in a ball on the floor?"

"No, of course not," she replies. "I need to know whether to call for paramedics. Give me a minute to figure this out. Please."

I narrow my eyes and adjust my nasal cannula. It became dislodged when I fell, but it's still there—mostly in place. "Dahlia, we've talked about this. Even if I am having a stroke. I don't want any extreme measures. No hospitals. No paramedics. No resuscitation. You promised me you'd respect my wishes."

She puts her phone in her pants pocket then wrings her hands as she looks at me. "I know, Ruthie. I promised. I do promise. It's just that seeing you so helpless is hard to take. Now that you want to reconcile with Meredith and meet Rosemarie, I feel an even heavier responsibility to keep you in good health long enough to make sure it happens."

"I don't think the phrase good health will ever apply to me again," I say. "Not in this body. Or this lifetime."

"Stop it. You know what I mean," she replies.

"Then start by helping me up, would you?"

Finally, Dahlia comes over and leans close so that I can wrap my arms around her neck. Her silky hair brushes against my cheek as she lifts me back onto my feet. I lean against her, grateful for the human touch.

My days tend to be lonely. A simple touch from a friend means so much.

The thought brings tears to my eyes as I wonder if I'll ever touch my daughter and granddaughter. If I'll ever be close enough to smell their shampoo and feel their silky hair. What I wouldn't give to hold them, even for a minute.

"There," Dahlia says, steadying me with one hand while repositioning my oxygen tank with the other. "Can you support your own weight?"

I sigh. My heart is racing, overexerted from the effort. "I'm not sure," I say, my face now wet with a salty mixture of tears and perspiration.

"Let's get you back in bed," she says. "Then we can

talk." She can tell I'm crying. It's embarrassing, but I can't help it.

I smile sheepishly, happy for even the possibility of Dahlia endorsing my trip to New Orleans. A part of me realizes that I'm in no condition to travel to the mailbox, let alone New Orleans. Another part is enthralled with the idea that there's a chance. There has to be some way for me to get down there. "Thank you," I say as she helps me to the bed. I keep one arm tightly around her neck.

"You're very welcome, Ruthie," she replies as she sets me down then helps me get comfortable. "I want you to have and do every single thing you want. Truly. I beg of you, though, think of the risks."

"What risks?" I situate myself and pull the soft comforter up to my chin. It's a security blanket at this point. I feel safest underneath its pale pink waffle weave. Maybe I can bring it with me on the trip. Maybe Rosemarie would like to have it when I'm gone.

Your time is running out.

The familiar refrain from the old Chaos roller coaster at Opryland hounds me now. I hear it in my head, a warning that the Grim Reaper is drawing near.

Dahlia sits on the side of the bed, but is too preoccupied to smooth her skirt this time. "Risks like getting overheated in the oppressive Louisiana humidity," she explains. "I've been down there. I know how hot and miserable it is this time of year. Or what if you fall and injure yourself because you're too weak to move around like you used to. I mean, gosh, Ruthie, you could even develop a blood clot from all the sitting and end up hospitalized in some random backwoods town along the way. What would we do with you then? Huh? This is serious business."

"I hear you," I say. "But what if none of those things happen. What if the worst thing to come of it is that I get extra tired and uncomfortable. I can live with that. Hell, even if I die weeks or months sooner than I otherwise would, my life is ending. The potential benefits far outweigh the costs."

"There are no guarantees—"

"Of course not," I say. "I'm well aware."

She pauses and looks at me, her eyes swimming with something I can't quite put my finger on.

I've never asked Dahlia for a favor. Nothing more than what she has offered. I've been careful to keep our bond clean. I'd hate myself if Dahlia grew to resent me. Meredith resents me enough. Rightfully so, but I don't want anyone else to ever feel that way. I certainly don't have time to repair new grievances. My hands are full with all of the old ones.

After a few silent minutes, Dahlia pulls her phone out of her pocket again, then cues up Rae's number. Her girlfriend's face grows large on the screen as Dahlia initiates the call and places it on speaker. I watch expectantly. I have no idea what Dahlia plans to say or how it will affect me. Maybe she wants Rae to bring me hot chicken. Or maybe ... I shouldn't speculate. Beads of perspiration form on my brow as I wait.

"Hey!" Rae says, her smooth, rich voice booming through the air. Her parents are from Mexico. Rae was born here in the States, but she has a subtle accent I've always loved.

"Hey, there," Dahlia replies. She stares at me while she talks. This is definitely something about my plight. It has to be.

"What's up?" Rae asks.

Dahlia takes a breath. "I'm here with Ruthie," she explains. "You're on speaker."

PART II
A FATE WORSE

6

———

SEEN

MEREDITH

New Orleans

"Hoist me up," I say to my husband, gesturing. Mitch has already gone in and Silas is on his way. I'm standing outside the metal railing next to our side porch. Shattered glass cascades down the stairs and I'm in bare feet. I don't want to be left out, though. I want to do my part. Especially since I might have prevented this whole episode from happening if I'd told anyone about the threats I received.

"There isn't time!" Silas shouts. "Wait here. Call the authorities."

I shake my head. "No cops."

My blackmailers were crystal clear about that. If I involve the cops, they say they'll hurt my family.

That's right. *Blackmailers.* The word sits heavy on my tongue.

My husband stops and turns to look at me, the shock evident on his face. "Are you out of your mind? A man just broke into our house, and he's in there right now with our daughter. We need all the cops. Call them!" I hesitate, but he pushes. "Do it now, Meredith! Make the call!"

I still don't answer and I don't intend to call the authorities, but Silas goes inside the house anyway. There isn't time to waste. I agree with that sentiment. "I'm right behind you," I say, grabbing the railing and hoisting myself over the side.

"Go away! Go away! Go away!" Rosemarie shrieks from somewhere in the distance. She sounds younger than she is, like a small child. Her repetition makes me imagine that she's in a fetal position, rocking back and forth. She's regressed, out of sheer fright. My heart breaks for her. It makes me think that maybe I should call for help. Yet, I can't. Not if there's any other option. We must handle this ourselves.

I need time to process the shock of seeing Mitch alive and in the flesh. And while I wouldn't admit it to anyone —not even to myself—deep down, I know what this man is here for. Maybe I'm paranoid and this is a random crime. Or maybe it's not random at all. If that's the case, it's imperative that I leave law enforcement out of it. The safety and future of my family could depend on using discretion today.

I hear a commotion in the kitchen as I make my way in through the door and to the adjoining mudroom. "Silas?" I call. "Mitch?" No one answers.

A dog runs past me at full speed. It takes a moment for her identity to register. It's Calliope. She's clearly scared to death, her posture low and coiled, searching for an escape. She runs out the side door so fast that I don't have any hope of catching her. I close my eyes and shake my head. Rosemarie will be heartbroken if anything happens to that dog. Thankfully, Alphie and Sara don't follow. They must still be in the house, trying to protect Rosemarie. Good dogs.

I move expeditiously, my eyes scanning for signs of a struggle. I cover the short distance to the kitchen quickly. When I get there, it's empty. The men must have moved on to another part of the house. "Rosemarie?" I call.

"In here, Mommy!" she replies, her voice shaky.

"Where?" I ask as I shuffle across the hardwood floors in the main hallway and scan each new room as I pass. Several areas are torn up as a result of the renovations taking place on our property. It takes extra time to search and clear those spaces. I comb through, careful not to miss any nook or cranny.

The bottoms of my feet feel raw. I must have stepped in a bit of glass, despite my efforts to avoid it. I tell myself that it doesn't matter. I'll tend to any cuts or scrapes later.

"The living room!" Rosemarie shouts.

All of a sudden, Alphie and Sara both begin to bark furiously again. Their woofs intermix with the sounds of doors slamming on the other side of the house, near the swimming pool. I ignore the clamor and focus on my daughter, picking up my pace. I'm almost to her. "I'm coming, baby girl. Hold on."

"Hurry!" she says fretfully.

When I round the corner to the living room and lay eyes on my child, relief washes over me. She's in one piece. She looks frightened, but unharmed. She's standing, so not in a fetal position, after all. "Oh, thank God," I say as I rush to take her into my arms. I kiss her forehead five times in a row, and she doesn't pull away.

"I'm—" she tries. She can't find words. This is perhaps the scariest thing that has ever happened to her. She seems to be handling it remarkably well.

"Shh," I say, "you don't have to talk right now. Are you okay? Are you hurt?"

She shakes her head. "I'm not hurt. Just scared."

I kiss her forehead again, lingering this time, savoring her sweet smell. "You saw the strange man run in here?" I ask.

She nods. "The strange man came first. He took your laptop. Then the smoking man—"

"Wait," I say, pulling back to look into her eyes. "The strange man that broke in here took my laptop? You saw him take it?"

So, my suspicions were correct.

"Yes, Mommy," she replies. "He rummaged around a little, but as soon as he found your laptop in your bag, he grabbed it and ran out toward the pool. The smoking man and Daddy ran after him."

"Fuck," I say. Rosemarie shoots me a look. "Sorry," I add. "Shoot."

"Should we make sure the doors are closed and locked?" she asks.

I nod. "Yes, good idea."

We go to the sliding doors leading to the pool deck, then we close them and make sure they're latched. We check the front doors and lock them, too, then we make our way to the place of entry with all the broken glass.

"How will we lock this?" she asks. "Anyone could come in."

I furrow my brow, remembering Calliope and her mad dash outdoors. She could be blocks away by now, or worse. Cars tend to drive slowly down Lakeshore Drive, but there's no way to know if the scared dog might dart in front of one.

I debate whether to tell Rosemarie the pup is missing. We need to make sure Silas is okay before we worry about the dogs. Even though she seems to be doing okay, my daughter might not be able to handle the ups and downs of what's to come. I want to keep things as even keel for her as possible. I decide to wait before saying anything about the runaway pup.

"Let's find Dad, and he'll know what to do about this broken glass," I say. "He can probably get one of his contractors out here to fix it. I don't think the reno team we've hired does glass. At least, that wasn't part of the scope of the project we negotiated. Dad's guys would probably be faster."

"Okay," she agrees, and we head back to the pool area where we last heard a commotion.

When we get there, Silas and Mitch stand facing each other, deep in conversation. Both look disheveled, but uninjured. There's no sign of the stranger who broke in and led them on a chase. There's an air of camaraderie between them. I'm not sure I like it.

"Rosemarie, wait here," I say as I move to unlock the glass door. It seems silly that we locked it in the first place, given the one hanging wide open on the other side of the house.

"No way," she says. "I'm not leaving your side. Especially not with that broken glass door unattended. How can we be sure that strange man isn't coming back?"

I'm conflicted, because I want—no, need—to have an adult conversation with Silas and Mitch. Yet, my daughter is still panicking. What kind of mother would I be if I shoved her away and ignored her feelings? I've been waiting for an opportunity to grow closer to her. This could be it.

"I need to talk to your dad," I say. "You stay right here on the other side of this door where you can see us and we can see you. You said it yourself—the strange man who broke in is gone, right?"

She nods. "I also said he could come back. And what about the smoking man?" she asks. "He's still here. A little while ago, you and Daddy were worried about him, asking me all kinds of questions like he was a big, scary threat. Make up your mind, would you?"

There it is again. A twinge of irritation on her part. A pang of longing on mine. I had better tread carefully here. My life could easily go up in flames—in more ways than one.

Before I can make a decision and answer my daughter, Silas notices us standing there and motions for me to come out and join him. I'm sure Mitch has been filling my husband in on all sorts of unsavory details of my past. Yuck. I'm hesitant to do anything but find a way to bury my head in the metaphorical sand like an ostrich, because it's beginning to feel like all roads lead to a disastrous outcome.

When I don't move right away, Silas opens the door.

"Meredith, will you join us, please? The intruder is gone. We chased him up Lafayette Street toward Claiborne. He hopped on a motorcycle and fled the scene. We're safe."

"Did you get a plate number?" I ask. I'm not sure why I ask, really. It just seems like the thing to say.

"A partial," Silas replies. "Along with a thorough description of the man and prints that can surely be pulled from in here, it shouldn't be hard to nab him."

"No prints," I say. "I mean, no cops, so no dusting for prints. We're all fine. Let's leave well enough alone."

Rosemarie and Silas both look at me like I have lost my everloving mind. Silas narrows his eyes. He's a pro when it comes to staying calm and keeping his reactions to a minimum. It's a skill that has come in handy countless times in our marriage. I always hate when he uses it on me, though. It makes me feel like I'm being managed, like I'm some diva celebrity or difficult customer. "Come on out," he says thoughtfully. "Introduce me to this long lost friend of your parents. He helped us today."

Upon hearing this, Rosemarie lights up like a Christmas tree. "The smoking man is a friend of Grandma and Grandpa's?" she asks, all traces of fear gone from her voice. She practically stands on her toes, her whole body lengthening with interest.

I let out a breath I didn't realize I'd been holding, and I steel myself for the inevitable. "Yes," I say. "Mitch here is an old friend of theirs. I haven't seen him in ages."

"Hello," Mitch says with a tentative smile. He shoves both hands into his pants pockets and looks like he might want to join me in my ostrich lifestyle, if given half a chance.

Rosemarie steps outside and wraps an arm around her dad's waist while she appraises Mitch. "See, Daddy," she says, "I told you he wouldn't hurt us. He was just watching."

I've been too preoccupied to track back on that aspect of this situation, but Rosemarie's comment reminds me how indignant I felt about a grown man talking to our daughter when no one else was home. Now that I know it was Mitch, I feel a little better. But still. What the hell?

Silas says what's on my mind. "Mitch, many thanks for what you did this morning, man. We appreciate you. So, I trust you'll give me an honest answer when I ask why you've been watching my home." He stands up straight, posturing to let Mitch know he's the younger, stronger specimen. He takes a step forward and puts a firm hand on Mitch's shoulder. "Why have you been watching my home?"

Mitch has always been a solid, standup guy as far as I've known. He doesn't shrink, which is why it surprises me when he slumps and breaks eye contact with Silas. "I'm sorry if I caused you folks any alarm," he says. "That's the last thing I'd ever want to do."

Mitch doesn't mention that he used to be a cop. That fact might ease Silas' mind. Or it might make him even more suspicious.

Silas swallows hard, his muscles tensing. "Understood. Now, my question?"

Mitch's gaze darts around as he scrambles to think of an acceptable answer. I can tell he doesn't intend to lie, but he doesn't want to reveal the truth, either. I want to know what he's doing sniffing around our house just as much as Silas does. But I don't blame Mitch for treading lightly. He somehow managed to find me after I went to great lengths to keep my old life in the rearview mirror. There must be an important reason for him showing up here, like this.

Alphie and Sara come traipsing over and sit by our feet nervously, providing a much-needed diversion. They seem amped up, still on high alert with their dog-sister missing. I take the opportunity to change the subject and throw Silas off Mitch's trail, even if only for a few minutes. I am genuinely worried about Calliope. Now that I know Rosemarie is okay, I want to find our pup.

"Has anyone seen Calliope?" I ask.

Rosemarie stiffens. "Not since that man was inside our house. The dogs were all three running around like crazy. Alphie was in the kitchen barking when the man was searching through things. Sara was barking, too. I don't remember when Calliope was. Have you seen her?" She peers into my eyes, awaiting an answer.

"I wasn't sure at first," I begin, "because everything was happening so fast, but I think she ran out the open door on the other side of the house."

"What?" Rosemarie says, instantly breaking into tears. Her face balls up. "And you didn't tell anyone until now? I hate you!" she shrieks. "You let our dog run away. She might get hit by a car … and she might die." She sniffles, then wipes her wet nose against one wrist. "If Calliope dies, it's all your fault!" she shouts.

My heart sinks.

So much for any progress the two of us have made. My daughter hates me.

"Hey, easy does it," Silas says, wrapping Rosemarie into a tight hug. "It's okay. Calliope knows her way around the neighborhood from all the walks we've taken her on. You know that, right?" He pulls back, then lifts Rosemarie's chin gently, encouraging her to meet his gaze. "We'll find her."

Mitch perks up, seemingly happy to have a mission. Men always like a mission, in my experience. I suppose his reaction shouldn't be a surprise. "She's the black and white dog, right? The setter." Silas nods. "I can help," Mitch says.

"You hear that?" Silas asks Rosemarie. "Now we have help. We'll find her."

Silas shoots me a look that says we have a lot to discuss later. I acknowledge him with my eyes, then I shift my attention to the two dogs at our feet. Priority number one now that the people are safe will be keeping Alphie and Sara from getting loose. "I'll secure the other two dogs in the pool house," I say. "You three go look for Calliope. Once I get Alphie and Sara inside, I'll stand watch at the open door in case Calliope comes back home before you do. Send me texts to keep me posted. Okay?"

Silas nods and Mitch gives me a hearty "10-4." Silas has, apparently, given up on his insistence that I call the police at this juncture. Rosemarie doesn't look my way.

"Go!" I say. "Let's not waste any more time. I'd feel terrible if something happens to our girl. I don't blame her for getting spooked."

"How about you make some calls while we're gone," Silas suggests. He doesn't specify what kind of calls he'd like me to make, but I'm a responsible adult. I get the picture. If there weren't extenuating circumstances here, I'd have already beaten him to the punch. And besides, I have some calls of my own to make. Calls that Silas doesn't necessarily need to know about yet.

"I hear you," I say, then I shoo the three of them out the front gate and onto Lakeshore Drive in front of the house.

I'm well aware that Rosemarie will use this time to ask Mitch a boatload of questions about my parents. I can't stop that from happening any better than I could stop day turning into night or the ebb and flow of the tides. I'm resigned to it now that Mitch is here. Now that my past has been torn wide open. Sadly, I need the time for myself. To tend to unsavory matters that have come home to roost. I'd hoped it wouldn't come to this. I'd hoped I could find a way out before my family became involved. No such luck.

I put the dogs away in the pool house as promised. They don't object, seeming ready to rest after the excitement they just experienced. "Be good," I say as I move to close the door behind me. Alphie whimpers once as if to affirm his understanding. "Calliope will be back soon … Silas will make sure of it."

Determined to conduct my inquiries before anyone returns, I pull out my phone on the way to the open door. As for call number one, I know the number. It's been memorized for an occasion such as this. I dial, my palms sweaty with apprehension.

"Peacheasy Interiors, Marley speaking," the receptionist says in a cheery voice.

Pride swells in my chest every time I hear our firm's

name. I picked it, nearly fifteen years ago when it was just Becca and me working out of my tiny apartment in Slidell. The life I'm living now was but a dream back then. I'm proud of what we've accomplished.

"Good morning, Marley," I say. "Is Becca in yet?"

My friend and business partner is notoriously low tech. She prefers to communicate via the landline phone on her desk instead of texting or talking on her mobile like civilized people do. I play along so as not to offend her. This conversation needs to be as rudimentary as possible, anyway. I don't intend to discuss anything serious until we're face to face and I'm sure no one else is listening.

"She's here!" Marley chirps. "I'll put you right through."

"Thank you," I say, then I wait.

Every ring feels excruciatingly slow as the seconds tick by. "Come on. Pick up," I mumble. Finally, she does.

"Mer?" she asks, her voice bright and eager. I can practically see her blonde hair sashaying around her shoulders, her freckles peeking out from below her blue rimmed glasses.

"It's me," I confirm, glancing around outside to be sure no one is listening.

"I thought you'd be in the office by now. We have the Eaton client meeting this morning. Remember?"

"I know," I say. "I'm sorry."

She can hear in my voice that something is wrong. "What's up?" she asks.

I sigh. "I was going to come in late this morning because Silas and Rosemarie wanted to go for beignets.

You know how tough it is to get in Rosemarie's good graces these days."

"Sure," she confirms. "I sense a 'but' coming."

I nod, even though I know she can't see me. "But there's been a change of plans. Or maybe a delay of plans. I don't know if we're still going for beignets this morning. Silas and Rosemarie are out looking for Calliope. She got out through the open door—the glass is broken."

"Slow down, Mer," she says. "Tell me what's happening."

I take another breath. Becca and I have a codeword chosen in the event that danger finds us and we need to speak in a secure location. I'd hoped and prayed that I'd never have to use it, yet here I am, about to. "I could go for some *pepperoni* pizza," I say, emphasizing the code word pepperoni. "Meet me there tomorrow?"

"Oh," she replies. "Oh, dear."

Becca knows that I'm not actually talking about pepperoni pizza, and she knows where to meet me. "Lunchtime?" I ask.

"Okay," she says. "I'll take care of the Eaton meeting. Enjoy the beignets with your family. I'll see you at noon tomorrow."

I agree, then hang up the phone. As the call ends with a chime, I get the uneasy feeling that someone is watching me. I turn, expecting Silas or Rosemarie—maybe even Mitch. Instead, I see a shadowy figure move around the far side of a large column. I stand, determined to see for myself who it is. I won't cower. Especially not in my own house.

I fill my lungs with air. "Who's there?" I ask loudly. There's no answer. Whoever this is must think they can hide. "I saw your shadow," I say.

It takes another minute, but finally, a familiar face emerges from behind the column. It's Magdalena Angelos, the woman tasked with managing our renovation project. She has a key to the house, so why is she skulking around like she doesn't belong here? She's been working on site for months.

"My apologies," she says, brushing a few strands of silver hair out of her eyes. She steps closer, her hands clasped and her body relaxing into a more normal posture. "I know I'm here earlier than usual this morning. When I arrived, I saw the broken glass and wasn't sure what was happening. Is everyone all right?"

"No worries, and no need to apologize," I say, without thinking anything of it. I ignore the uneasy feeling in the pit of my stomach. "We're shaken up, but I think we'll be just fine."

"Good," she says. "I'm glad to hear it. If I can help in any way, please let me know. Will you be calling someone to take care of the glass?" She raises a hand in the air and points in the direction of the breach. "Or should I?"

Magdalena crosses her feet at the ankles as she stands, an unusual pose for a woman who is normally an open book. It's as if her body is confused as to how comfortable it is. I can't help but wonder if she's hiding something. I've never thought anything remotely like that about the woman before.

I tell myself that I must be paranoid. Maybe the

heightened emotions are taking more of a toll on me than I initially realized.

"I think Silas' guys can handle it," I say. "I'll keep you posted."

We chit chat for a few minutes, then Magdalena excuses herself to get back to work.

"Have a lovely day," she says. "Enjoy the sunshine and try not to let what happened this morning stress you out. You're loved and cared for—by more people than you know."

"Will do," I say with a smile.

If only it were that easy.

7

———

TEAMWORK

RUTHIE

Nashville

"Oh, hey, Ruthie!" Rae says cheerfully. She's a lovely young woman, every bit as nice as Dahlia. They make a great couple.

"Hey, Rae," I reply. "How's work going today? Anything interesting to share?"

Rae is an interior designer, like the rest of us. She and Dahlia met in college at Savannah College of Art and Design in Georgia, then moved to Nashville together after graduation. Rae is currently working for a firm that specializes in commercial interiors. She's a whiz at computer aided drafting and is finding her footing managing large-scale projects. I'm proud of her.

"I'm still working on the new hotel going up in the Gulch that I told you about the other day. The one with owners who want guitar-themed everything, yet they want it to be classy, with a hearty dose of Southern charm. I'm not sure that's possible," she says with a laugh. "I hope it doesn't turn out too gimmicky. I'm doing my best."

"I believe you are," I say. "I've never envied you commercial interior designers. There's so much more pressure to strike the right tone, and everybody and their mama is bound to have an opinion about it. At least, with our residential clients, we only have to please one family. It seems much easier."

"Understood, my friend," Rae says. "You know what they say—opinions are like assholes."

I laugh, then continue the saying. "Everybody has one."

"And they usually stink." Rae adds, laughing, too. I enjoy our easy rapport. "So," she says, moving on, "how are you doing this morning? Keeping my girl Dahlia busy, I assume?"

Dahlia's been listening quietly, but she jumps back in. "Um, Ruthie had a bit of a tumble in her closet while trying to get a suitcase out," she explains with one brow raised. "She has big plans. She's been packing, and making secret phone calls that she thinks I don't know about."

"Well, to be fair, the closet thing was more of a slide than a tumble," I add quickly.

"Okay, then, let's just say she spent time on the floor, until I helped her up," Dahlia clarifies. "Is that fair?"

I shrug.

"What's this all about, Ruthie?" Rae asks. She sounds louder than before, as if she's leaning closer to the phone. "We don't want you to go and injure yourself. That would be uncomfortable for you, and tough for everyone taking care of you. Picture it—casts, rehab, pain, and so on. You know what I'm saying?"

Rae stands up for Dahla without hesitation, and I admire her for it. I like the way they have each other's backs. "I know," I say. "I promise I do. There are special circumstances that made me want to get my suitcase."

"And make secret phone calls," Dahlia adds.

"Oh?" Rae asks, her interest piqued. "Are you planning to go somewhere?"

"You've got that right," I say emphatically. "Dahlia hasn't told you?"

"Told me what?" Rae asks.

Dahlia shakes her head.

"I thought maybe she called or texted you when she left my room a little while ago," I explain.

"Ruthie, dear," Dahlia says. "I was changing laundry loads during that time. I'm not sure you realize how long the chore takes."

My face crumples, feeling badly. "I'm sorry," I say. She already took wet sheets off my bed this morning and replaced them with fresh, clean ones. If it weren't for her, I'd have bedsores by now from allowing urine to eat away at my skin. I hear that can get ugly real quick.

I hate that I'm incontinent. It doesn't even make sense to me the way my body is failing. It's an endless cascade of one problem after another, all thanks to my damned heart. It's true what they say about not realizing what you've got until it's gone. I sure wish I could somehow go back to good health. To driving myself again. To working. To independence, as a competent adult.

Dahlia shakes her shoulders and her head, "No, I'm

sorry. Forgive me. That wasn't nice of me to say. I'm happy to help you, Ruthie, as long as it takes."

As long as it takes for me to die and get out of everyone's way, I think. My self esteem recovers quickly, though, and I shrug the negativity off. There's too much to be excited about, if I can live long enough to see it all sorted.

Your time is running out.

"She knows how dedicated you are, Dahl," Rae adds.

"I do," I confirm.

There's a pause, but Rae quickly fills the air. "What's the trip?"

I brighten again. "Remember that private investigator I hired to track down my daughter?"

"Of course, I do," Rae says, her voice still close and loud in the phone. "Did he find Meredith, one hundred percent for sure? Oh, my God, that's spectacular, if he did!"

"Indeed he did," I say happily. "She's living in the New Orleans area. Mitch says she's married to a good man who looks a lot like my Pete. And get this—I have a granddaughter!"

"What?!" Rae exclaims. "No way! Ruthie, that is the most amazing thing I've heard in a long time. How old is she? What's her name? Spill the tea!"

I practically squeal with excitement. Rae's energy is contagious. "She's fourteen and her name is Rosemarie," I say. "That's all I know, but I want to meet her and find out more." I inhale sharply, afraid I've gotten ahead of myself. I'd hate for Rae to feel coerced or pushed. I'm not angling for her and Dahlia to take me to New Orleans. Although, I wouldn't mind if they did.

"Lovely," Rae says. "Rosemarie is a very beautiful name."

"That's what I said when I heard," Dahlia adds.

"I think so, too," I say, "but I might be biased."

We're smiles all around, basking in the glow of my happy news. After a moment, Dahlia proceeds. "Ruthie wants to go to New Orleans right away," she explains. "To meet Rosemarie and attempt to patch things up with Meredith. She wants to take special things with her in the hopes of passing them down to Rosemarie."

I want to do a lot more than that. I *have* to do a lot more than that. I must make up for what I've done. I decide to keep those details to myself, for now.

"Yeah?" Rae asks, the wheels in her mind clearly turning. "Has Mitch made contact with them yet? Have you, Ruthie?"

"Not yet," I say. My heart sinks again. I know it won't be easy to convince Meredith to speak to me, let alone to allow me to meet Rosemarie. My daughter has been hiding from me for many years. Come to think of it, she disappeared around the time she would have met her husband and become pregnant. Sadness fills my face. Dahlia notices.

"Ruthie, a penny for your thoughts?" she asks.

I can't help but smile at the old fashioned phrase. I get a kick out of the sayings Dahlia comes up with. Sometimes, I wonder if she researches them ahead of time, just to make me happy.

"I was doing the mental math," I reply. "It's been fifteen years since I've spoken to my daughter. Fifteen years since I knew anything about her life, including where she lived. I'm guessing her decision to start a family of her own was the impetus to cut ties with me. It stings."

Dahlia takes my hand in hers and gives it a squeeze. "What's done is done," she says softly. "Let's focus on the future, okay, my dear?"

Talk of the future makes me instantly panicked. Heat rushes to my neck and my heart skips another beat. I don't want to be a bitter old woman droning on about how little time I have left, but …

Your time is running out.

I'm twitchy. Restless. I want to get started on my packing. It feels like it's time to *do* something, not sit around and yammer on about it. But I must be patient. I'm in no position to do any of this on my own.

"Do you think Meredith will talk to you?" Rae asks. "I mean, if she knows your situation, maybe she'll give you a chance to explain, right?"

"I honestly don't know," I say. "What I did to her is unforgivable. I wouldn't blame her if she refused to speak to me ever again. My heart would break—hell, I'm probably dying of a broken heart right now—but I wouldn't blame her. My daughter's life is forever changed as a result of my choices. She can't go back and regain her innocence. She certainly can't bring her dad back. I took him away from her."

Dahlia and Rae both know what I did—at least, they know the generalities. I told them the basics months ago, when I first entered hospice and Dahlia offered to take care of me. I felt an obligation to be open and honest with them about my past. They reacted with a surprising amount of kindness and compassion. I only wish I could find the same compassion for myself. If Meredith never forgives me, how can I forgive myself? It's a tangled, complicated mess. I decide to focus on one step at a time. Step number one is getting my fragile body to New Orleans.

"Like I told you earlier," Dahlia says, "as long as you're here, living and breathing, there is hope. You can't give up."

I nod, grateful.

Dahlia turns her attention back to the phone. "Rae, Ruthie wants to hire a driver to take her down to New Orleans. Do you know anyone?"

"Hmm, let me think," Rae says, playing along. We all know what Dahlia is talking about. "I'm not sure I know a driver for hire, exactly, but I happen to have a lot of vacation time built up. And I do love New Orleans. The music, the food, and the history draw me right in."

"I didn't realize you'd been there," Dahlia says.

"Yeah, I was there once as a kid, then I went with a few friends on a senior trip the summer after we graduated high school," Rae explains. "It's a fun place."

"I've never been there before, but I wouldn't mind checking out some of the historic homes in the city," Dahlia says. "Maybe get some design inspiration that I can use in future projects. Nashville and New Orleans seem to share certain sensibilities, even though they each have their own distinctive vibe."

"That's not a bad plan," Rae agrees. "Maybe I could find some inspiration for this guitar-themed hotel project. New Orleans might just provide me the oomph I'm looking for that can be brought back home and brought to life in Nashville's Gulch."

"I can see how that might happen," Dahlia replies. "It could be a working trip, of sorts, for us both."

My eyes grow wide as saucers and my brows shoot up. I've been listening, but I can't sit quietly any longer. "I can pay!" I blurt. "I have lots of money."

Dahlia looks stern, like a mother scolding a rambunctious child. "Ruthie Flores, we aren't after your money," she says.

"Oh, I didn't mean it like that," I reply, feeling like an ass. "Not at all. I just mean that I have plenty of money to pay for whatever we might need on the trip. I'd rather have my health, believe me. I'd trade every last cent for a good heart that would allow me to stay alive another ten years to watch my granddaughter grow up. In that span, I might see her graduate college. Maybe she'd even fall in love and get married." Tears spring to my eyes again.

"I know, my dear," Dahlia says, softening. "I know."

I grab a tissue from the bedside table and blot at my eyes. "I hate being a blubbery mess almost as much as I hate being so damn weak due to a failing heart," I say. "You ladies are too good to me."

Dahlia smiles warmly and pats my hand. "It's okay. The truth is, neither of us will have the chance to take care of our own mothers like this. Mine is gone and Rae's is meaner than a snake. As long as Rae is gay—and I promise you, she is—her mother won't even claim her. So, Ruthie, darling, perhaps taking care of you fills something in us. Did you ever consider that?"

I shrug slowly. I hadn't thought of it that way. I knew

Dahlia's mom passed when she was a kid. Ovarian cancer took the woman within weeks of them finding out about it. Dahlia was nine, and I'm not sure she'll ever fully recover from that kind of loss at such a young age. She and her mom were very close. As for Rae's mother, I knew she didn't take it well when Rae came out, but I guess I didn't realize the full extent of her disdain for what she considers a lifestyle choice. It hurts my heart to see these ladies longing for a caring mother figure in their lives. I'm honored to fill the role, if they'll let me.

"Spoken like a wise woman," Rae adds. "She's right, Ruthie. Totally. You can put any guilt or bad feelings you have to rest where we're concerned. Let us help you. It's an opportunity for us to do something meaningful. It's our privilege. I promise you, it is. Seeing you hug your daughter's neck will be reward enough."

"You don't think I'm a bad person?" I ask, feeling like a scab over my very soul is being prodded and picked at. I don't like talking about this, but I also don't like *not* talking about this. Better to air it out, I suppose.

"Absolutely not," Rae says. "You are not a bad person, by any stretch of the imagination. What happened was an accident, plain and simple."

"Public opinion would tend to disagree," I reply. "I'm sure there's an angry mob somewhere that would still like to see me burned at the stake."

"No, I don't think so," Rae says, getting fired up. "For Christ's sake, Ruthie, you didn't go to prison because those jurors *knew* it was an accident. That's all the public opinion that matters."

I twist a clump of blanket absentmindedly as it all

comes flooding back. The bloody scene, Pete's body on the ground so still and cold, the arrest, and the trial. The memories have been tucked away in my mind, but they return in vivid color. It doesn't seem to matter how many years pass. That trauma stays perpetually fresh, fueled by Meredith's insistence on making sure I'll never put it behind me.

I wonder if Mitch still thinks about it.

"Good point, Rae," Dahlia says. "The jury set you free, Ruthie. Besides, that was a long time ago. What good will it do to keep punishing yourself? You rebuilt your life after that mess. You took care of yourself, supported your daughter through college, and built a successful business. You've done all anyone could."

"Did you read any of the newspaper articles?" I ask sheepishly.

"Yeah, we did," Dahlia replies without hesitation. "You didn't tell us enough to make finding coverage easy, but based on the timeline and location, we pieced it together. The fact that the other man involved was a drifter seems to have helped keep the story lower profile than it might have been otherwise."

"He wasn't exactly a drifter," I say. "That isn't an accurate description."

"Have *you* read the articles?" Rae asks me.

I sigh. "A long time ago. That's ancient history, remember?"

"You tell me," Rae replies. She's more feisty than Dahlia. More assertive. I don't mind.

"Do we really need to rehash this now?" I ask.

"No, we don't need to rehash anything," Rae says.

"You brought it up. You asked if we think you're a bad person. We don't. It sounds like you might feel that way about yourself, though, and that's a shame. I'd sure like to see you let the past go. To forgive yourself."

I blurt without thinking it through. "How can I forgive myself when there's something big Meredith still doesn't know? Something that would make her hate me even more and prevent her from ever truly forgiving me."

Your time is running out.

I hadn't told them about this part. No living person knows. Not a soul.

"What's that?" Rae asks. "Is there something else, Ruthie? Something you haven't told us."

Guilt and shame wash over me like a raging river. As if someone flipped a switch, I move into panic mode. My chest tightens, my heart clenched so tight it feels like it might clank and thump right out of my body. Beads of perspiration form on my brow and my hands become clammy. My respiration becomes labored. I can't seem to get a full breath. My vision tunnels.

Is this what a panic attack feels like? Or am I having a heart attack? A stroke? Maybe Dahlia was right, the checklist be damned. Will my New Orleans trip be over before it starts?

Dahlia moves closer, concern all over her face. "Ruthie, what's wrong? Are you feeling okay?"

I peer at her, but can't get enough air to speak. My breathing becomes short and jagged. I pant, like an animal.

"Rae," Dahlia says, "call 9-1-1. Something is bad wrong here. We have to get help."

"No!" I manage. I don't want paramedics poking at me. Even if I die here and now, today, I want to go out on my own terms. I need Dahlia and Rae to respect my wishes. "No interventions. No resuscitation. No extreme measures." The words come out in fits and starts, but they come, nonetheless.

The three of us sit quietly as we wait to see how things will play out. Rae stays on the phone. Dahlia holds my hand and gently wipes my brow. It takes nearly twenty minutes, but I finally calm down. My chest finally relaxes. My breathing slows. The color comes back to my vision.

"I'm not ready to talk about it," I say, when I finally work up the strength to speak.

We all know what I'm referring to. Thankfully, Dahlia and Rae respect my privacy and don't ask any questions. I'm sure the questions will come later. I can't drop a bombshell like that and expect no one to mention it again.

"That's all right, Ruthie," Dahlia says. "Don't you worry about a thing. We can talk later."

I'm not sure I want to reveal my secret—ever. Perhaps I should take that little tidbit to the grave. No one would be the wiser. I'm far too exhausted to decide right now. The morning's excitement has left me plumb tuckered out.

"There is something I want to share, though," I whisper. "I've come up with a plan. The Southern Charm Society …"

I must be mumbling, because they can't make out what I'm saying.

"What did you say?" Rae asks.

"Something about her arm?" Dahlia wonders. "Is

your arm okay, Ruthie? Is it the one that was hanging funny?"

"I'm sorry," I say as I lean back against my soft pillow. "I can't keep my eyes open. I—" I begin to drift off before I can finish my sentence.

On my way into a deep sleep, I hear Dahlia and Rae talking in the distance. Dahlia has moved into the hallway outside of my bedroom, but she leaves the call on speaker. "I don't know how on God's green earth we're going to accomplish it, Rae, but we have to take this woman to New Orleans," she says.

"Agreed," Rae replies. "Consider it done. I'll talk to my boss. As soon as you can, start packing."

8

WATCHED

MEREDITH

New Orleans

It's hot and muggy when I arrive at Moxie Tavern the next day. I park in a city lot two blocks away, turn off my phone, then hurry inside so as not to be seen. Though there's little breeze today, Hank has the windows wide open. I can't imagine it any other way. Wide, open windows and doors are part of the French Quarter charm we all know and love.

"Water with lemon *and* lime," I say to the waitress as I slide into a booth in the back and remove my wide-brimmed hat and sunglasses. She smiles and heads to the painted-black bar to do as I've asked. She must be new because I don't recognize her. I suppose that's a good thing. I needed some distance from this place.

I sit facing the front so I can be sure to see Becca when she comes in. The air conditioner is pumping earnestly in this part of the dining room. Blessed cold air tousles my hair and frames my face.

"Thanks," I say when the water is delivered. "I'll wait to order lunch until my friend joins me. She'll be here shortly."

"Any apps?" she asks, her nose ring glistening under the dim overhead lights.

The juxtaposition of the low light in this part of the tavern and the bright, almost blinding light streaming through the front windows a short distance away is familiar, to say the least. There's a life metaphor in there somewhere. I'm too stressed to find it.

I tilt my head, considering what I might be able to stomach right now. I'm still full from the leftover beignets I ate this morning, but realize I need something more substantial. I ate beignets yesterday, too. They're better fresh. "Do you still have chips and guac?"

The waitress nods and returns to the bar where she keys in my appetizer order, then leans over and absentmindedly wipes a gold handrail affixed to the front. That thing gets filthy with spills and sticky fingerprints. I know, because I've cleaned it myself hundreds of times— maybe even thousands. I lost count.

Being here makes me remember all sorts of things.

The sounds of the city, the smell of horses as their carriages shuffle tourists up and down the bumpy street out front, the raucous parties that spill into the wee hours of the morning, the Mardi Gras beads and costumes ... they all swirl in my mind. Then there are the handsome, devilish men from around the world, here for a drink, and sometimes more.

I lived out my wild days inside the walls of this tavern. Many nights, after my shift, I had hot, sweaty sex in one of the two small bathrooms positioned directly across from where I'm sitting right now. It was another life. Another world. I was acting out and finding myself, all at once. This city. This neighborhood. This tavern—and Hank Baugh—they took care of me.

"Right on time, Meredith Flores," Hank says as he sits down and makes himself comfortable. "Good to see you, kid."

Although I haven't been called by my maiden name in ages, Hank's voice is music to my ears. I hadn't thought about it until now, but maybe he filled the honorary uncle role that Mitch vacated, way back when. "Good to see you, too, Hank," I say.

He pulls a vape pen out of his pocket and fires it up.

"They let you use that thing in here?" I ask, waving my hand in front of my face. I don't want to breathe in and coat my lungs with that nastiness, but in all honesty, my body has been subjected to far worse. I'm somewhat surprised I made it through my twenties without any permanent damage. Perhaps the damage just isn't evident yet.

"Shit, are you kidding me?" Hank asks. "During the height of the pandemic, the City of New Orleans required us to check vaccination status before we could let paying customers inside. Hell naw, they don't let me smoke in here."

"But you're doing it anyway, you rebel," I say with a grin. "Good ol' Hank. You haven't changed a bit."

"I push the limits where I can," he says proudly. "Life's a lot more fun that way."

We both know that the lunch rush hasn't hit yet. The

city is slow to wake up each day. Hank has at least fifteen more minutes to smoke his heart out before anyone who might report him gets here.

"How's business?" I ask. "My server seems good. Is she taking proper care of things?"

Getting the idea we're talking about her, the young woman glances our way. She quickly drops her gaze when Hank makes eye contact. "Kristin? Yeah, she's good. Business is good. You know how it is—there are slow days, but the crowds never stop coming to NOLA. The pandemic took a bite out of us, for sure. We're still alive and kicking. Business hasn't dried up, if that's what you're asking."

It suddenly strikes me that Kristin probably isn't more than four or five years older than Rosemarie. *I* wasn't much older than Kristin when I worked here. It seems too young. The realization makes me nervous. I tap my index finger on the table in front of me as I eye a sign on a nearby column that says no persons under twenty-one are allowed. I've always thought it strange that you can serve alcohol when you turn eighteen but can't drink or hang out in bars in your free time until you're twenty-one.

"Good," I say. "I'm glad to hear it. It's been a while since I've been here in person, but I check in on you."

"Is that right?" he asks, his bushy silver goatee moving as the vape pen reaches his lips. "How do you check in on me? What, do you have spies sneak in on Saturday nights when I'm too busy to notice?"

I chuckle. Hank isn't exactly a modern man of the times. He spends most of his life in this tavern, not out in the world learning about the latest technology. The only reason he has a presence online is because one of the owners of the restaurant next door helps him with it.

"No need for spies, silly," I reply. "I check your Facebook and Instagram pages. Customers tag you in a lot of photos, which makes it easy for me to keep tabs."

"Is that so? Huh."

"I like to look at photos of this place when I'm feeling nostalgic," I say.

It's hard for me to believe sometimes, but I kept a go-bag back in those days. I was ready to flee at a moment's notice. To where, I'm not entirely sure, but I stayed ready. Marrying Silas and having Rosemarie changed me in certain ways. Growing up was unavoidable. It's a good thing. It's just—I don't know—odd to think about the new and the old melding together. What's been gained?

"Are you feeling nostalgic now?" Hank asks.

I meet his gaze. This man knows me. It might be an old version of me that he's best acquainted with, but that doesn't matter much when it comes down to it. The core parts of my personality haven't changed. I'm still the same hopeful girl, determined to craft a life of my choosing rather than wallow in the one my mother left in her wake. Hank knows my history. The gist of it, anyway.

"I'm nostalgic now that I'm here," I say.

"You weren't before?"

"I don't know. Maybe a little more than usual the past couple of days," I explain. "An old family friend of my parents' showed up at my house out of the blue yesterday. He met my daughter."

"The big, pretty house on Lake Pontchartrain?" Hank asks. He hasn't seen it in person, but he's heard about it. I showed him a photo on my iPhone once, not long after Silas and I first moved in.

"That's the one," I confirm. "I'm not even sure how he found me. It's been fifteen years since I've spoken to … *her*."

I hear the disdain in my voice. It sneaks out like a viper that has been awakened after a long sleep. My anger is still hot and raw, at its core. I wish I could forgive my mother and let our history go. I've tried—meditation, yoga, pilates, talk therapy, and even a sweat lodge experience in the woods of Washington State—but no luck. The bad feelings towards her remain.

"That still troubles you, kid?" he asks as he finally extinguishes the smoke. "I'm sorry to hear it. I hoped you'd put that b.s. behind you by now. You've built a good life for your little family. You deserve peace."

To that, I smile big. I've tried. It's been the most important endeavor of my life. It might not feel like it to Rosemarie when I'm at work a lot, but I work hard for her. So that she can have a better childhood than I did. So that she can navigate her young adult years without the kinds of burdens I carried.

"Thanks for saying so," I reply. I don't tell him about the trouble I'm facing now. Not yet. "I know you've always wished things were different with your ex-wife and your daughter," I add. "Has your relationship changed now that your girl is grown?"

"You know," he says, his brows raised, "I'm working on that. I actually wrote her a letter. Want to read it?"

I do, but Becca should be here any minute and we have very serious things to tend to. How can I refuse the man, though? He was there for me when I needed him most. The least I can do is read his letter and offer a few kind words of encouragement.

"You bet I do," I say as Kristin drops a basket of chips and a ramekin of guacamole on the table. I grab a set of glass salt and pepper shakers from a small metal basket and season my food, then I dip a chip in some guacamole and delicately bite an edge. My stomach is too upset to feel genuinely hungry. I might have to nibble if I want to get anything down.

Hank leaps out of his seat, pleased that I've agreed to read the letter. "Be right back," he says. "I'll go get it! You'll be proud of me. I swear it's good. And I'm not just saying that. A therapist helped me figure out what to say."

"Okay," I manage, chewing slowly. Hank disappears into the back room just as Becca walks in the front door. "What timing," I mutter. I wish I'd had a chance to read Hank's letter before moving on to whatever this conversation holds for me.

Becca bounces when she walks, despite the serious subject matter we're here to discuss. She sees me almost immediately, and I wave her over. She, too, is wearing a hat and sunglasses. She takes the shades off and slides them onto the collar of her silk blouse as she sits down across from me in the seat Hank just vacated. She keeps her hat on, which seems dramatic. Or touristy. Either way, she looks the part.

"Hey there, Bec," I say. "Nice hat."

She pauses, unsure if I'm being sarcastic or not. "You didn't wear a hat? I thought that—given the pepperoni pizza nature of this meeting—we should keep a low profile."

I reach over to the booth beside me and lift my hat to show her. "Oh, I wore one. I just took it off when I sat down. That's all." A small smile turns the edges of her lips upward. "You look good," I continue. "I'm out of sorts. Don't take my remarks too seriously."

She narrows her eyes, much like Silas does when I say something strange. "Why do you feel the need to explain?" she asks. "You okay, Mer? You don't seem quite like your usual self."

Perhaps Becca doesn't know me as well as she thinks she does. Or more likely, she doesn't realize how much trouble I'm in. How could she? "I'm fine," I say. "At least, I will be fine. Once I handle some snags that have presented themselves."

She stretches her arms out in front of her like she might crack her knuckles. She stops short, then folds her hands in her lap. "Are we going to jump right into it? No small talk—or food—first?"

"Have a chip," I say, pushing the basket her way. I take one and dip it in the guacamole, then pop it into my mouth. "I'm not sure I'm hungry," I add, "but I figure I should eat. So ...?"

"Thanks," she says. She smiles, relaxing a bit. I can tell she wants to ease into this, so I'll oblige.

"How was traffic on the causeway?" I ask.

She shrugs. "I wasn't far behind you, was I?"

"No, Bec," I say, lowering my brows. "I'm making polite conversation. Go along with it, please."

"I see," she replies with a scoff. "Well, traffic was fine.

It's a pretty day out there. The sky is bright and blue. Lake Pontchartrain is calm. There are no tropical storms headed our way at the present moment." She pauses, remembering. "Oh, and there were a slew of sea birds perched on top of the little police buildings that dot the Causeway Bridge. What are those called?"

"The birds? Or the buildings?" I ask.

"The buildings," she replies. "Are they outposts? Towers? Causeway doohickeys? Whatever they're called, I've always wondered if they have bathrooms in those things or if the folks who man them have to piss over the back railing, into the lake."

At this, I laugh so hard I spit a chunk of tortilla chip onto my shirt. Becca knows how to ease the tension, and I appreciate her for it. "I've never given much thought to what those little buildings are called," I say. "No one explained them when I moved down here. I suppose I didn't think to ask."

"I'd look them up online," Becca says, "but you insisted I turn off my phone before entering the tavern. Want to tell me what we're doing here?"

There she is. I knew it wouldn't take my feisty friend long to get down to business. "I thought you'd never ask," I say.

Before we can dive into the meat of the matter, Kristin returns with a tentative smile on her face and takes Becca's drink order. Becca forgoes any healthy choice and opts for sweet tea. She also orders mozzarella sticks, claiming that she's famished. I suppose she might as well enjoy herself while she can.

When Kristin leaves, Becca develops a change of

heart. "On second thought, let's eat our lunch before we talk about unpleasant things," she says. "I'm digging the vibe of this place. I'd love to soak it in and hear about how you know the owner."

"Okay," I agree.

As if on cue, Hank appears from the back room. He's gripping a white envelope for dear life. His weathered face is joyful, his shoulders high with pride. When he sees Becca at the table with me, I can tell he isn't sure how to handle it. Our arrangement includes privacy, but I'm comfortable with both Hank and Becca knowing my secrets. Most of them, anyway. By that measure, my friends might as well know each other.

"Speak of the devil," I say to Becca. "Here's Hank, now." I motion for him to come over and join us, then I slide over in the booth so that he can sit down beside me.

"I hope I'm not interrupting," he says sheepishly. Hank has always been good about keeping his nose out of people's business. The flip side is that he's hesitant to become privy to anything sensitive.

He hands me the envelope and I drop it into my handbag for safekeeping. I'll read the letter later.

"Not at all," I say, patting him on the back. "Hank Baugh, meet my friend and business partner, Becca Vincent."

Hank smiles politely and extends his hand to shake Becca's. She reciprocates, her eyes searching for the backstory on our unlikely friendship. "Nice to meet you," she says.

"Likewise," Hank replies. "Any friend of Meredith's is a friend of mine."

"The two of you go way back, do you?" Becca asks.

Hank looks to me to tell as much or as little as I'd like. "Way back," I confirm. "Hank is one of the first people I met when I moved to New Orleans. He gave me a job as a waitress. I lived in a tiny studio a few blocks away while I got my shit together and decided what to do with my life."

Becca's brows raise. "Really?" she asks. "You worked *here*?"

"Don't sound so shocked," I say with a laugh. She kicks me under the table playfully. "You know what I mean," she adds.

"Meredith Flores is one of the best employees I've ever had," Hank adds appreciatively. "When she left, it was my loss."

"You're sweet," I say to Hank, then I purse my lips and consider how much to tell Becca. She fills the pause.

"Meredith Flores, huh?" she asks.

I've never told Becca my maiden name. She only knows me as Meredith Montgomery. Although my legal name is actually Meredith Flores Montgomery. I've been able to use just Montgomery for business documents.

Hank looks worried. "Oh," he says. "I'm sorry."

I stop him. "It's okay. I go by Montgomery now. Flores is my maiden name."

Becca's eyes narrow again. "I don't mean to pry. I … well … I thought you graduated from college in Savannah, Georgia before you came to New Orleans," she says, working to piece things together. "Savannah College of Art and Design, right?" I nod. "That's one of the top colleges for interior designers to attend. You were poised for a stellar career, which you're now having. I guess I don't understand the pit stop after college. Why did you go to work at a bar—?"

"A tavern," Hank says.

"Right, a tavern," Becca continues. "And a lovely one at that, I might add."

Hank smiles at the compliment. "Thank you."

"It is pretty nice," I reply. "Classic French Quarter charm. No place else like this in the world. I won't say I enjoyed every minute of serving drunk tourists, but all things considered, my time at Moxie Tavern was one of the best in my life. It was a reprieve when I needed it most. It provided me a place to hide away from my horrible mother. So, there was that."

Becca nods, but she looks skeptical. I get the sense that she'll ask me plenty of questions when the two of us are alone. Putting a pin in it for now is fine with me.

Kristin delivers the mozzarella sticks and refills our drinks, allowing for a break in the conversation. "That was fast," Becca says.

"Sure was," I say. "The cook must have had these mozzarella sticks prepped and ready to drop into the fryer when the order came in."

Hank smiles. "They're hand breaded, too."

Becca and I taste the fried cheese, then compliment Hank on how good it is. The food here has always been excellent. Searching for a change of subject, my gaze falls to the floor. I'm not sure whether I want to tackle the elephant in the room, even though I know I'll have to do so soon. Kristin hasn't taken our lunch order yet, so I have a little time.

"Hey, did you find Calliope yesterday?" Becca asks, still chewing cheese.

Hank looks confused, so I clarify. "One of my dogs," I explain. "She got out yesterday morning. Actually, someone let her out when they broke in."

"What?" Hank asks, stiffening.

"Yes, though," I continue, "she came back and was locked safely in the pool house with her siblings, much to my daughter's relief."

"Did you get the beignets?" Becca asks.

Hank shoots Becca an astonished look before he can stop himself. She ignores him.

"We did," I confirm. "Silas was able to get one of his contractors out right away to fix the door. Plus Magdalena, the lady overseeing our renovation project, arrived at the house not long after everything happened yesterday morning. She stayed on site to watch over the place."

"Good," Becca replies.

I talk with my hands. "Silas, Rosemarie, and I went for beignets then took Rosemarie to school. She arrived late, but I don't think she minded one bit. I would have let her stay home yesterday and today, except that I had to hatch a recovery plan and come here. Besides, home might not be the best place for her to be alone. I don't think any of us got much sleep last night."

"Well," Becca says, "you've been talking about remodeling that side of the property to add a carriage house and covered drive anyway, right? Maybe this is the nudge you need to extend the reno project further."

"Wait, back up," Hank says. "Who broke into your house?"

"I'm not sure," I say, and it's the truth. "Some guy who seemed to be after my laptop. Rosemarie said he searched like he knew what he was looking for, then took off once he had my computer in hand. He got away with it."

"Is that what this meeting is about?" Becca asks. Hank eyes me, interested.

I shift in my seat. "Yes," I say simply. I'm tempted to hem and haw and to make excuses, but I don't.

"Do you know what he might have been after on your laptop?" Hank asks.

"Yes."

He eyes me suspiciously. "Does this have anything to do with your mom?"

I'm shocked. Not at his suggestion, but because he actually hit the nail firmly on the head. How did he know? I glance down at the table, avoiding eye contact. "Why do you ask?"

He puts one meaty palm down in front of me. "Call it a hunch and humor me. Does it?"

Becca looks intrigued. She takes a sip of her sweet tea and waits for me to answer.

"I want nothing to do with my mom," I say. "I don't want to talk about her."

I raise a hand into my hair and tug. Within seconds, I realize it's the same motion Rosemarie uses when she's anxious. The same motion I criticized her for. *Damn.* What kind of mother am I, anyway? I should be a better one. I drop the hand.

Hank removes his palm from the table and wraps it around his expansive chin. He looks like an old, wise man in this pose. "Look here, Meredith, you've got to get a hold of this thing, or it will take hold of you. Do you catch my drift? You're in the middle of something ugly. I can feel it."

I meet his gaze. "I haven't spoken to my mom since before my daughter was born," I say. "My mom doesn't know where I live. I'll fix this. I promise. I won't let her derail the life I worked so hard to build."

"You aren't making much sense," Hank says. "I'm sorry to put it that way, but I don't know any other way to put it. I'd like you to fill in some blanks for me."

I purse my lips then open my mouth to speak, but nothing comes out.

Becca leans forward. "Mer," she says, "are you in financial trouble? Is that why this concerns me, as your business partner? Do you need a loan from our company? Do you want me to buy you out? Because otherwise, I'm not sure what I'm doing here."

Before I can say anything else, I notice a man at the bar staring at me. He's been there for at least a few minutes, but he came in behind a group of others and I assumed he was with them. He looks vaguely familiar. I think I might know him. I scan my mental Rolodex to try to place his face and match it with a name.

Hank sees my concern. "Do you know that guy?" he asks.

"No," I reply. "Do you?"

"No."

Becca turns to look. When she does, the man turns

away to avoid our gaze. Upon seeing the back of his head, it clicks. "Oh, fuck," I say.

"What?" Hank asks. "Is he bothering you? Want me to get rid of him?"

I nod vigorously. "Would you?" I ask.

Hank moves to stand. He's heard all he needs to for now. Before I can stop him, he heads to the bar. He's protective of this place, and of me. As much as I pride myself on being an independent woman who doesn't need a man to take care of her, I'm grateful.

Becca wants to learn more. "Mer, who is he?" she asks. When I hesitate, she presses. "Tell me."

I sigh, my nerves becoming frazzled by the implications. I lean forward and lower my brow. "That's the man who broke into our house yesterday morning," I say. "He must have put a tracker on my car."

9

____

LEARNING MODE
RUTHIE

Nashville

I t's evening when I wake up. I'm disoriented at first, the low light confusing to my weary brain. Apparently, I missed most of the day. I'm not sure what time it is. The excitement took a lot out of me. After a few moments, I remember everything that's happened—Mitch's call, New Orleans, and my granddaughter.

"Bloody hell," I say, the expression feeling odd as it comes out. I stretch and rub my bleary eyes.

"Bloody hell?" Rae asks, amused. "What, are you British now, my dear?" She's reclined in an easy chair next to my bed, reading a novel on her phone.

"Rae, you're here," I say softly.

"Where else would I be?" she asks. "We have a trip to prepare for."

I prop myself up on one elbow, then notice a puddle of drool that has dampened my pillow case. My bottom is damp, too. I must have wet the bed again. I put a hand on my chest and feel my heart drumming away inside like a clunky motor running on fumes. It seems the failing organ is working overtime.

I'm not as confident about traveling as I was this morning. My body shut me down when I got overexcited by a phone call and a minor fall in my bedroom closet. What will it do on a road trip so far away given all of the unexpected things that could occur? If I can't make it to New Orleans alive and breathing, all of my effort will be for nothing. I won't get to see my daughter or meet my granddaughter.

"I wonder if I should find another way," I say. "Maybe I was too hasty earlier. I'm not in good condition."

"I know," Rae replies. "You're doing okay. It isn't over yet. But that wasn't earlier today."

"It wasn't?" I ask.

"Nope," Rae replies. "That was yesterday morning. You've been sleeping for more than twenty-four hours. Something like twenty-seven, to be more precise."

My eyes widen. "Holy shit," I mumble. It's all I can think of to say. I knew I'd been sleeping more lately, but I didn't realize I could be out of it for quite this long. It's mind boggling. What was I doing all that time? What were Dahlia and Rae doing?

Dahlia hears us talking and enters the room. I'm embarrassed to tell her that the bed she changed for me is wet once again. "Hello, Ruthie," she says sweetly. "How did you sleep?"

"Like a rock," I reply. "I was dead to the world." We all bristle. Why do I keep saying such insensitive things?

"You've been sleeping hard, that's a fact," Dahlia says.

She walks to the side of my bed, then stops short. She probably smells the urine.

"I'm sorry," I say. "I can't help it. I wish I—"

"Stop," Dahlia says. "It's a natural part of life. Don't you apologize."

"You mean a natural part of death," I say. "Life, not so much." I sigh. "I never would have guessed that pissing myself would go along with the dying process. It's not like I have bladder cancer. How does heart failure turn into all of these other unpleasant symptoms? Not to mention, it's so much urine that the damn incontinence underwear won't hold it. How does that happen? I'm a petite woman."

Dahlia shrugs. "I'm not a nurse so I don't know for sure, but you slept a long time. I imagine anyone sleeping for so long would produce a lot of urine. We could ask Anne if you like. She'll be here bright and early tomorrow morning."

I shake my head. "I'm just thinking out loud. Don't worry about it. Help me up, would you?"

She does, then she strips the sheets off my bed and takes them to be laundered while I go into the bathroom to get clean. It takes every bit of my energy to slowly wash my body in the shower and to put on clean clothes. When I return to the bedroom, I'm famished. I must look hungry, because Rae reads my mind.

"Ready for some dinner?" she asks, setting her phone on a dresser and standing to meet me.

"I could eat," I say, trying to make light of the situation.

"Take my arm, my dear, and I'll escort you to the

dining table. We have something we think you'll like," Rae says.

I smile. "You and Dahlia are too good to me," I reply just as the scent of hot chicken reaches my nose. "Hattie B's?"

"You know it," Rae says while we walk. "I heard you had a hankering for the one and only Miss Hattie Bishop's famous Nashville hot chicken. My wish is your command. I picked some up on my way home from the office. I got fried pickles, pimento mac & cheese, and banana pudding, too."

My mouth practically waters. "All of my favorites," I say. "Although my favorite dessert is a toss up between banana pudding and peach cobbler. Both are to die for."

Rae chuckles, so I don't apologize for the death reference. Maybe it's becoming my trademark thing. Better to joke about it than to stay so serious that people have to walk on eggshells around me, I suppose.

"Did you bring me some of their sweet tea?" I ask.

Rae nods. "I wouldn't forget such an important part of the meal. What do you take me for?"

We laugh together as we walk slowly, my slippers making soft thuds against the creaky hardwood floors. I've often thought of replacing these floors, but could never bring myself to tear the old material out. It's original to the house, which was built in the 1920s. They don't make them like this anymore.

When we arrive in the dining room, Dahlia has the table set as if we're having a formal dinner. She pulls out a wingback dining chair at the head of the table, then Rae helps me sit down and get comfortable in it. The ladies work together to push me in, then Dahlia places a crisp cloth napkin on my lap. The napkin is so neatly pressed, I wonder if she ironed it. I glance around at the place settings and notice that my best silver is on display, polished to a bright shine. Candles are lit and placed along the midline of the table. A bouquet of pink and white hydrangeas from my garden sits proudly in a glass vase nearby.

My house looks gorgeous, if I do say so myself. I've always been proud of how nicely it's decorated. It's a true designer's showplace. What a shame that I won't be around to enjoy it much longer. If I could, I'd stay right here.

"Would you look at this?" I ask with a smile. "Fine dining tonight. To what do I owe the pleasure?"

"Are you complaining?" Rae asks. "From where I'm sitting, I'd say you lucked out this evening. You've got Hattie-B's, and you didn't even have to fight Nashville traffic."

I shake my head and wait. They're up to something. They have to be. There's no other explanation for all of this. Don't get me wrong, the ladies take good care of me every single day, but this is different. Something is different.

"Hot chicken, coming right up," Dahlia says as she fetches the dinner trays from the adjacent kitchen. She's wearing the same heels she had on yesterday morning. It makes me wonder if she's been home at all since then. The heels clink as she walks on the wood floors, quieting only when she reaches the table and steps onto the jute rug that lies underneath.

"Smells delicious," I say. "I'm ravenous."

"Good," Rae says. "Then you'll be happy to dig in along with me." She scoops heaping portions onto my plate, then hands me the salt and pepper shakers. "Eat up!" she says.

We eat hungrily, every single bite tasting like heaven as it slides down and warms my belly.

The hospice folks tell me I'll lose my appetite soon, and that my body won't need food anymore. I haven't reached that point yet, but I can sense it coming. It's unsettling, to say the least. I intend to eat as heartily as I can until it happens. Now, granted, sometimes I'm too sad and depressed by my predicament to feel like eating much, but during times like tonight when I have good food and good company, I'm able to enjoy it.

When Dahlia finally slows down, she dabs at the corners of her mouth then looks deep into my eyes like she's proud to have provided me with a good experience. "You seem to be pleased," she says. "Is Hattie B's as good as you remember?"

I smile broadly. "Better," I say between bites of mac.

"I'm so glad you're happy," Dahlia coos.

Without thinking it through, I add, "the only thing that could make this evening better is having Meredith and her family in those empty chairs next to you."

Now that I've said it, there's an impetus for Dahlia and Rae to do something about my request. I didn't mean to heap more onto their shoulders. I was simply expressing my feelings.

Rae leans back in her chair and places her napkin on

the table in front of her. "Wouldn't that be nice?" she says as she eyes Dahlia.

I get the idea they've discussed me while I was sleeping. I'm sure they do it all the time, but this evening, it seems like something more. "It sure would," I reply. "I don't mean to ruin a good thing, though. This is lovely. Thank you."

Dahlia is the mediator. The fixer. She grabs my hand and gives it a squeeze. "Ruthie, don't you apologize for saying what's on your mind. We want you to speak freely around us. We want to make your wishes come true."

I look at Rae for confirmation. "We do," she says, tilting her head to one side. "Whenever possible."

We make small talk about my garden as we eat dessert. Dahlia mentions how pretty the hydrangeas are. Rae says she looks forward to seeing my mums bloom, come fall. We all know I probably won't be alive to see that happen. We talk about it anyway. It feels good to have a normal conversation with my friends. For a little while, I forget my troubles and immerse myself in the simple pleasures of a good meal and interesting conversation.

When we're finished, Rae clears the table and loads the dishwasher, then asks me which other restaurant I'd like her to bring takeout from. The promise of a trip to New Orleans hangs in the air, as does my rapidly declining health. None of us knows for sure if I'll be here and feeling well enough to eat takeout on another evening. I tell her I'd love some food from The Loveless Cafe, though it's on the far west side of town and not on Rae's path home from work.

"Loveless is amazing," Rae agrees. "Those homemade

biscuits and preserves are incredible. They're far better than Cracker Barrel's biscuits, and that's saying something because Cracker Barrel biscuits are scrumptious."

"I agree," Dahlia says. "My favorite dish at Loveless is the pork chops. What's yours, Ruthie?"

"I was always partial to their meatloaf," I say. "It was Pete's favorite. On weekends, we used to ride out to The Loveless Cafe on his motorcycle for lunch, then meander along the Natchez Trace Parkway for a lazy afternoon. Autumn along the Trace is glorious. Spring is pretty nice, too." Warm feelings wash over me as I remember. "One time," I continue, "we saw two little donkeys—at least, I think they were donkeys—trotting side by side on a stretch of the Trace between Nashville and Franklin. We slowed down to marvel at the unusual sight, but those little donkeys kept right on going. They were moving fast, like they knew what they were doing and weren't bothered by us. I hope they made it home okay."

They nod and smile, happy to share in my memory.

"Hey, speaking of Pete," Rae says. "We wanted to talk to you about something."

I stiffen. Here it comes. This can't be good.

Your time is running out.

"Oh?" I ask. "What's that?"

Dahlia shifts in her chair, but Rae stays steady and sure. "Mitch called," Rae says.

I wrinkle my nose, a visceral reaction to his name. Within seconds, though, I remember what a gift he's given me by finding my Meredith. I tell myself to relax. "When did he call?"

"While you were sleeping," Rae continues. "He called twice, actually."

"Why didn't you wake me up?" I ask, frustrated. "I want to talk to him. He might have more information about Meredith and Rosemarie."

"We tried to wake you up, Ruthie," Dahlia says. "We tried hard. You were sleeping like a log and wouldn't rouse. You barely stirred."

I find this hard to believe. Not that I don't believe them … it's just that I've always been a light sleeper. I wake up if a plane flies overhead or a bullfrog gets chatty. How could I possibly have slept so hard—for twenty-seven whole hours—that Dahlia and Rae couldn't wake me? That doesn't make sense. "That's strange," I say simply. "I'm not usually such a deep sleeper."

"I know, my dear," Dahlia says. "I thought it was strange as well. It worries me, truth be told. Things might be … progressing."

I wave my hand in the air. "It's probably fine," I say. "I'm probably fine."

Your time is running out.

"I hope so," Dahlia says. The sincerity in her voice is evident. It's touching to hear.

Moving on, I want to know about Mitch. "Did you talk to him?" I ask.

Rae nods. She's clearly the leader of the couple. Dahlia doesn't seem to mind the supporting role. There's an ease between the two of them. "We did," Rae confirms. "With so much going on and such high stakes, we decided to speak openly to Mitch. I hope you don't mind."

I do mind. Yet I also don't. I don't know. There's no perfect solution here. Only a path of least resistance. "Go on," I say, raising a hand to my mouth and twisting my bottom lip. Nerves threaten to get the better of me. There's a tangled history between Mitch, Pete, and me that's dramatic enough to rival any daytime soap opera. These young ladies have no idea the can of worms they might be opening.

"He says he talked to Meredith in person yesterday," Rae says cautiously. "Says he talked to Rosemarie and her dad—Meredith's husband, Silas—too."

"What?!" I ask, incredulous. Heat flares on my neck and my stomach tightens into a knot. "He shouldn't have done that. He'll scare her off. Oh, God, why did he do that? I swear, that man. He makes me livid! Why can't he leave well enough alone? We were making headway. Now, my chance is probably shot. Thanks for nothing, Mitch Weller!" I shake a fist in the air as I rant.

Rae and Dahlia look at each other. They clearly have something more to tell me. They're afraid of my reaction.

"It sounds like he didn't have much choice," Rae says, her voice measured.

"What does that mean?" I ask. "Did Meredith recognize him? Did she remember him and know who she was talking to?"

"Yes," Rae replies. "Mitch says she introduced him to Silas as a friend of her parents."

I shake my head. "This can't be happening," I mumble. "Now Meredith will know that *I* know where she's living. She'll react strongly, no doubt. She'll take steps to keep me away from her family. I'll never get to meet Rosemarie. I'll never—"

"Ruthie, dear," Dahlia says, interrupting my downward spiral, "take a breath. You don't know any of that. Go *easy*. For the sake of your delicate heart, try to stay calm. Okay?" She pats my shoulder lovingly, then scoots her chair closer to mine. She's offering me much-needed emotional support. I'm too worked up to properly thank her. All I can do is nod.

Rae takes a breath and tries again. "Mitch told me that he and Pete were close friends," she says. "Best friends."

"At one time, they were best friends," I say. "They grew up together on Long Island. Then their friendship fell apart. Damage was done that couldn't be repaired."

"What kind of damage?" Rae asks.

I narrow my eyes and wave a hand in the air again. "Serious damage. I don't want to talk about it. It isn't my story to tell, anyway. Why do you ask?" Dahlia and Rae glance at each other once more. It's quick this time, but I catch it. "What?" I probe.

Rae touches her fingertips together and looks solemn. She's wearing a silky blue vest that bunches under the strain of her outstretched arms. "I'm not sure how to tell you this," she says.

"Now you're scaring me," I reply. "I've never known you to be at a loss for words, Rae Pate. What is it? Spit it out."

"Don't be scared, Ruthie," Dahlia implores. "Everything will be okay, one way or another."

"One way or another?" I focus on Rae. "Come on. What?"

She crosses one leg, changing her body position along with her approach. "How much does Meredith know about the day Pete died?" she asks.

Alarm bells sing in my mind. This isn't good at all. In fact, my entire world may come crashing down around me. Maybe *I'm* the one who should have left well enough alone.

"Um, she wasn't there when he died, if that's what you're asking. She was away at college. She attended Savannah College of Art and Design, just like the two of you. Only she was there a number of years prior." I keep talking in the hopes that I can change the subject and throw them off the scent. "She was twenty-two and in her final semester when Pete died. All of her classes were finished, but exams remained. Her professors were gracious about giving her time to attend her father's funeral and then sit for the exams when she returned to town. I worried that some of them wouldn't let her take the exams late, but they all did. She finished the semester strong with four As and one B. Can you believe that?"

They give me space to talk as much as I want. They're determined to get to the bottom of whatever it is on their minds, though. I can tell that much for sure.

"Understood," Rae says. "My SCAD professors were always kind and generous. I'm glad the college took good care of Meredith in her time of need. I'm also impressed with her fortitude. Not everyone could withstand that kind of trauma and continue to take care of business. Sounds like your girl is a lot like her mother."

I blush at the compliment. "That's nice of you to say," I reply. "I always thought Meredith was a lot like me. She's like Pete, too, of course. You can't grow up with a parent and not have some of them rub off on you. It simply isn't possible."

Rae tilts her head. "Why did you phrase it like that?" she asks.

"What do you mean?"

"You said you can't *grow up* with a parent without them rubbing off on you."

"Yeah? So?" I ask. I hear what she's getting at. I don't like it.

"Why wouldn't you say something about inheriting personality traits instead?" Rae asks.

Dahlia raises a hand and begins to chew on one fingernail. I've never known her to be a nail biter. The stress must be having a negative effect.

"Potato, po-tah-to," I say. "It doesn't mean anything. Unless you want to debate the whole nature versus nurture thing. I took a psychology class in college. Granted, that was a long time ago, but I watched a documentary on the subject recently. We can discuss it, if you like."

Rae pauses and Dahlia holds her breath. We're all silent as we wait to see who wants to push the issue. Finally, Rae softens, giving in. "Forget it," she says. "I'm sorry if I was overeager. I want the best for you, Ruthie. That's all."

I smile graciously. "Thank you," I reply. I wonder if she realizes how close she came to forcing the secrets out of me. I'm desperate to know what Mitch said, yet not at the expense of having my dirty laundry aired against my will. I want to do this on my own terms.

I turn and stare absentmindedly out the window. We can see my garden from here. It looks lovely in the evening light, a golden hue gently blanketing the flower petals and tops of the leaves. The sun is low in the sky and will dip below the horizon soon. The rolling hills in the distance will graciously take in the sun as it retreats for another quiet night.

"Ruthie," Dahlia begins, "are you tired? Do you want to lie down? We could watch some TV together in the living room, or I can help you get settled in bed."

I sigh. We haven't talked about so many important things that need to be discussed. It feels like torture—the hoping, the waiting, the worrying.

Rae answers for me. She speaks to Dahlia while peering into my eyes. "She isn't ready for bed yet," she says. "She slept a lot. Mostly, though, she has a lot on her mind."

I nod. "That's right. I do," I reply. "I don't know where to start. Or what to say."

In my head, I know exactly where to start and what to say. I want to know what Rae thinks I might not like to hear. I want to know what Mitch said when he called. Most of all, I want to know if they'll take me to New Orleans. None of that seems unreasonable to ask. I'm torn, though, because I don't want to be presumptuous. I am well aware of how vulnerable and precarious my position is. I certainly don't want to make things worse by dredging up the past when it has no real bearing on the present. If it isn't too much to ask, I want to pick and choose what comes to light and what doesn't. Besides all of that, I don't know if my frail body will allow me a quiet evening without trouble, let alone a big trip. I have serious concerns that I can't ignore, no matter how much I might like to.

Dahlia studies me. "You're deep in thought, my dear," she says. "Tell us what's worrying you. What can we do for you?"

I fidget, unsure of what to do. "I wish I knew," I say. Then I reconsider. "You know what? Screw that. I don't have time to pussyfoot around."

Dahlia's eyes widen and Rae cracks a big smile. "That's more like it," Rae says.

I carefully scoot forward in my seat and glance from one of them to the other. "You can begin to help me by telling me what Mitch said. I'm a big girl. I can handle it."

Dahlia sighs. "Are you sure?" she asks. "Can your heart take it?"

I close my eyes and steel myself. "Give it to me. Do it fast, like ripping off a bandage."

"Okay, then," Rae says. She pauses ever so briefly, then breaks the news as gently as she can. "Mitch called because he thinks Meredith is in danger."

I open my eyes and whip my head around in her direction. "What? What do you mean? What kind of danger?" I grip the arms of my chair so tightly you'd think I was on an airplane about to fall right out of the sky. My knuckles turn white, but I barely notice.

"He isn't sure," Rae continues, "but he was watching her house yesterday morning when a man broke in. Mitch leaped into action and eventually helped Silas run the guy off."

My heart pounds hard in my chest as blood swishes in my ears. "Why didn't you tell me this earlier?" Why did you let me eat a leisurely dinner and make smalltalk, when you knew?"

"Because everything is under control—for now," Rae says. "The immediate threat seems to have passed."

"Are you sure?" I ask. I have a million questions. I hate feeling so removed from my daughter and granddaughter's lives.

Rae and Dahlia both nod.

"They're safe for now," Rae continues. "They spent last night at home, but barely slept. So, the family has decided to stay at one of the vacation rental properties they own until they're sure it's okay to go back."

I breathe a sigh of relief. "Phew," I say. "That's good to hear." I try to imagine what Rae's conversation with Mitch must have been like. I chew my lip as I weigh the possibilities. "What can I do?" I ask. "I must do something. I absolutely *must*. You can't expect me to sit around quietly while my family is in danger."

"It isn't that simple, Ruthie, dear," Dahlia says. "I don't have to tell you that. You said yourself that Meredith won't exactly welcome your involvement in her life. You can't just barge in as if nothing's happened between the two of you."

"Maybe you're right," I reply. "Okay, fine, I know you're right. Which means I'll have to come up with a more creative solution. Actually, I *did* come up with a more creative solution. An old college friend has agreed to help pull it off. She just so happened to be in the right place at the right time. I have to call Magdalena back to get an update."

I swing my head from side to side, feeling on fire, in a good way. I'm full of energy.

"Wow," Rae says.

"I remember now that I was trying to tell you about my plan before I went to sleep … Southern Charm Society …" I muse.

They look at each other, curious, but skeptical. I know I'm rambling. I try, in earnest, to collect my thoughts and articulate them coherently.

"Okay," Dahlia says. "Let's hear it."

"You see, I've got to get eyes and ears into the situation so that I can figure out how to help Meredith and her family," I continue. "Now that Mitch's identity has been discovered, I'm all the more sure that my plan is the right thing. It can't be Mitch that gathers insider information for me. Not him alone, anyway. Meredith will push him out and away, just like she's done to me. She might not hate him as much, but she'll know that he's talking to me and she'll freeze him out."

"I'm sorry," Dahlia says. "I hate to see you suffer like this."

"Thank you for your compassion," I say. "But I'm not sure you're listening. I have a plan! It's already unfolding, as we speak."

"What's your plan?" Dahlia asks.

I lean forward and rub my temples, wracking my brain. I have to figure out all the specifics if I'm going to pull this off. Not to mention, I need to sound credible if I want Dahlia and Rae to believe in me. I'm going to need more of their help.

"It sucks being so limited," I complain. "So handicapped. I won't let that stop me though. I won't give up. Now that I know Meredith, Silas, and Rosemarie might be in danger, I have to figure out a way to help them. I have to implement my plan. It's an absolute necessity. If it's the last thing I do, then so be it. At least, this way, I can die in peace knowing that I've done something to redeem myself in my daughter's eyes. Something that will make my granddaughter think of me as a hero instead of a villain."

They stare at me. "Okay," Dahlia says again. "What is Southern Charm Society?"

"I need a notepad," I reply. "I can make notes. A bullet point list, maybe. It will all make sense if I can write it out. I can explain. Will you get me a notepad?"

Rae looks at her girlfriend, then back at me. She seems hesitant to change the subject, but an idea has sparked in her mind. Maybe an idea to piggyback on my idea? She seems somehow lit up. "Ruthie, grab your sweater. How about we go for a little ride?"

10

———

UNSURE

MEREDITH

New Orleans

"I'm being blackmailed," I blurt, unable to hold back the emotion in my voice. I blot at my eyes as the words topple out.

We're gathered around the expansive farm table in our property on Louisiana Avenue as the sun sets over The Big Easy. Luckily, no one had booked the house for tonight. It was vacant and ready for us when we arrived. According to the calendar on the vacation rental site we use to manage reservations, we aren't expecting guests for another week. It's a good thing, because my family needs a safe haven. I'm not sure our house in Mandeville is secure, even with the glass door repaired.

Silas picked Rosemarie up from school, then they got the dogs and drove down from the North Shore, stopping only for a carryout order at High Hat Cafe. The locally-owned restaurant is our go-to when we're in this part of the city. It seemed like comfort food was in order, given the day we've all had. The smell of smoked roasted chicken, delta tamales, BBQ shrimp, and slow roasted pork wafts through the open living space.

This house is long, front to back, and narrow with a big porch. One renter wrote in an online review that it felt like staying in a box car. She isn't wrong. Granted, it's a well decorated, luxurious box car. My design savvy is a huge advantage when it comes to setting up vacation rental properties that travelers will keep coming back to. This house is a gem, if I do say so myself.

I slather pimento cheese onto a cracker and stuff it into my mouth. It's a wonder I can eat at a time like this.

"You have to be kidding," Silas says, his shoulders heavy under the burden of my news.

"Does blackmail mean what I think it means?" Rosemarie asks tentatively. "Like what it means in the movies?"

Becca looks at my daughter sympathetically. "Aww, sweet girl," she mutters.

Becca doesn't have kids of her own, and she isn't always sure how to interact with the younger set. I hope she isn't too uncomfortable. I insisted that my friend spend the night. If I have it my way, Becca will stay right here until we know for sure it's safe for us all to return home. There's plenty of room, and we can't be too cautious.

"It's complicated," Silas replies, "but yes, I'm sure that's what it means." He looks at me. "Isn't it, Meredith?"

I nod, still chewing.

Alphie, Sara, and Calliope lounge at our feet, but they keep a watchful eye on the front door. They aren't sure what we're doing here. They can probably tell this isn't exactly a happy occasion. Dogs pick up on that kind of thing. They read the vibes in a room with the expertise that only comes from countless years of the evolution of their species. Or maybe it's our facial expressions they're reading. Either way, they know things aren't normal. Alphie pants nervously. I reach down and give him a quick scratch on the head.

"Your mother will have to share the specifics with us," Silas continues. "I assume that a bad man is threatening to say or do something mean if we don't cooperate and meet his demands. In a nutshell. Maybe they're after money. Greed is a terrible thing. Sometimes, wealthy people like us become targets simply by being in the wrong place at the wrong time."

Silas won't sugarcoat the truth. I wouldn't dare ask him to. I'm the reason we're in this mess. He shouldn't have to lie to our child about it.

Hank's been silent, sitting solemnly at the far end of the table. I don't blame him. He's just met Silas, Rosemarie, and Becca for the first time today. He doesn't want to overstep.

Rosemarie turns to me, resentment in her eyes. "What did you do?" she asks.

Hank leans forward and raises a finger as if he wants to defend me. He stops when I shoot him a look. We're long past the days when he needed to come to my rescue, even if I did ask him to get rid of the guy at the bar this afternoon.

"That's a really long story," I say. "I didn't do anything, exactly. It's more like I've found myself in the middle of a difficult situation."

Rosemarie rolls her eyes dramatically. "That low-key sounds like bull to me."

"Low-key?" Hanks asks, apparently unable to help himself.

Silas eyes Hank warily. My husband has had to become acquainted with two father-figures from my past today. Both were previously unknown to him. He's still adjusting.

"It's something teenagers say," I explain. "It means you don't want to come on too strong."

"Sort of, but no," Rosemarie says curtly. "It's more like actually, or for real. As in, that sounds like bull, *for real*, Mom." She moves her shoulders in rhythm to emphasize the words.

Hank is missing out on the bratty teenage phase of his daughter's life. An evening with Rosemarie might make him glad for unanswered prayers. Not to talk badly about my girl, but these teenage years are hard. *Low-key*.

"Should she be here for this conversation?" Hank asks.

We all look his way and wait to see who will be the heavy. He's my old friend, so I take on the role. "Yes, she should," I say. "Rosemarie is a bright young lady. She was dragged into this thing when a strange man broke into her house and scared her half to death yesterday. She has a right to be here."

Rosemarie smiles at me, appreciating the vote of confidence. Here we go again with the oscillating. One minute I'm the devil and the next I'm her savior. She's hot and cold. It's nearly impossible to tell which way the pendulum will swing next. There's no rhyme or reason. "Thank you, Mommy," she says.

Boy, she sure knows how to hit me where it hurts. *Mommy.*

Silas looks on approvingly. He likes it when we get along. I can tell, though, that he also wants me to start talking. I have a lot of explaining to do. In hindsight, I probably should have confided in my husband much, much sooner.

"Look," I say, fingering the pendant around my neck absentmindedly. The pink tourmaline stone set in gold was a gift from my mom on my sixteenth birthday. I'm not sure why I still wear it. "I know you all have questions. You're here because you're somehow affected by what's happening. We all want to get back to normal life as soon as possible. The truth, though, is that I don't know much. Not yet. In fact, my next step is to find someone who can help us get to the bottom of this."

"Like the police?" Silas asks. He knows I don't want to involve the police. We've already been over the topic. I wish he'd let it go.

"No police," I say.

He purses his lips. "Meredith, honey, the police aren't bad guys. Their entire job is to help keep law and order. Why are you so opposed to, at least, filing a report?"

Hank folds his arms across his brawny chest. He almost looks like a lumberjack in the pose. "I'm sorry for interrupting, Mr. Meredith," he says.

"Silas. Silas Montgomery," I clarify. "I don't think my husband wants to be called Mr. Meredith any more than I want to be called Ms. Silas."

Becca chuckles, easing some of the tension in the room.

"Understood," Hank says. "My apologies." He clears his throat and begins again. "Silas, in my world, police often *are* the bad guys. Not all of them, of course. Most are good. But I've lived in this city nearly all of my life, and I've owned Moxie Tavern for much of it. I learned early on to steer clear of the boys in blue whenever possible. Corrupt cops are a scourge on the City of New Orleans. I suspect it's the same story on the North Shore where you live."

"I know that's true, Hank," I add. "I remember you telling me some of your war stories back when I worked at the tavern."

Hank pauses and takes a breath, then addresses my husband again. "If Meredith doesn't want police involved, I trust she has a good reason."

Before Silas can respond, Rosemarie jumps in. She scrunches her nose. "Mom worked at a tavern?"

"I was as surprised as you," Becca says. She's not helping, but I suppose she's not hurting either. I'm willing to allow a diversion to pass some time.

"That's right," I confirm, happy to talk about my waitressing days rather than the much more important matters at hand. "After college. Before I started my interior design business."

"You mean, before *we* started *our* interior design business," Becca clarifies.

"Yes, that's what I meant to say," I confirm. "I did a short stint as a junior designer for Pendleton & Wright in between working at the tavern and meeting Becca, but it all happened within a short period of time. Less than a year, if I remember correctly."

It used to irritate the fire out of me when my mom would go off on a tangent to avoid a tough subject. I swore that when I grew up and had kids of my own, I'd be different. Now, would you look at me? I'm avoiding tough subjects with the best of them.

I don't want to be like my mother. She's a hard woman to love. I hope to God that I'm different. I hope I'm better. I gather my fortitude and let the conversation veer back toward what's important. We'll have plenty of time to talk about my early twenties on another day. A day when no one is in imminent danger of being shaken up—or worse —by an intruder.

"How come you never told us that?" Rosemarie asks.

"There are things in my past that I wish had been different," I say. "I wanted to wait until you were old enough to understand before I told you about them."

My daughter softens ever so slightly, but reaches up and tugs on a clump of hair. "Did you tell Daddy?" she asks.

"About working at the tavern?" I ask. She nods. "He knows. In fact, I was still working there when we met." I look at my husband. "Tell her, Silas."

He opens his mouth to speak, but Rosemarie is connecting dots quickly. "If Daddy knew you when you worked at Hank's tavern, then why hadn't they met each other until today?" she asks. "Shouldn't they have met each other?"

Hank smiles broadly as the connection dawns on him. "Wait a minute," he says, shaking a finger in the air. "You must be the hotel guy. Right? I remember hearing about you. You inherited hotels from your father when he died.

You were up and coming in the local scene when you and Meredith got together."

Silas smiles with a mixture of pride and what seems like apprehension. I can't quite get a read on his mood. "That's me," he confirms. "I had inherited from my dad and was finding my footing in the hotel business when I met my lovely wife. I like to think I've done him—well, both of them—proud."

"I'm proud," I say with a quiet smile.

Silas is sitting beside me. I slide a hand under the table and give his knee a squeeze. He moves his leg ever so slightly in my direction. It's enough to let me know we're still united. He isn't too angry with me, yet. I need his support, now more than ever.

"I should have known that was you," Hank continues, nodding at Silas. "I guess the link didn't dawn on me, but it all makes sense now."

"Now you know," Silas adds. "I'm pleased to meet you."

I smile at Hank as he looks at Silas approvingly. I want the men in my life to like each other. I hate to say it, but a part of me wishes Mitch could be involved in this little meeting of the minds. I've spent many years trying not to think about him. Seeing him yesterday brought so many memories rushing back. The man was good to me. I'm sure I can count on him. He proved that once again.

"Well, isn't this the touching scene?" Becca asks.

To a casual observer, this probably looks like a normal dinner party. No one would know the level of stress coursing under the surface. No one would realize that we aren't exactly here by choice. No one would see through our pleasant conversation to what lies beneath.

The group is quiet and I can sense that it's time for me to start talking. Seriously, this time. Diversions can only last so long. "I guess you want to know more," I say tentatively.

"That would be great," Silas says. "Anytime."

They stare at me, and heat rises on my neck. I finger the pendant again.

"Why are you fiddling with that?" Rosemarie asks. "Are you nervous? You always tell me to leave my hair alone when I start pulling on it. Seems like you might ought to take your own advice. You'll yank that stone right off your neck if you keep it up."

Little does she know that I was tugging on my own hair earlier.

Silas chuckles, admiring his daughter's spirit. Hank does, too, and the men share a knowing glance.

I drop the pendant and let my hand rest on the table. "What?" I ask.

"She's so much like you," Hank says. "You do see it, right, Meredith?"

"*Please*," Rosemarie says dramatically, emphasizing the vowels. "I'm nothing like her. In fact, I take after my dad."

Her comment hits me like a punch to the gut. My daughter doesn't want to be like me. *Ugh.* I look forward to surviving the teenage years, somehow. I *hope* we all survive them.

"Moving on," I say. "I'll tell you what I know."

A car zooms by on the road out front, loud music blasting from its speakers. This isn't the best neighborhood. It's fine. But the crime rate is much higher than it is on the North Shore. It's important that we remain vigilant, for more reasons than one. I pause as I debate whether we should close the blinds so as not to be seen. Our silhouettes will probably be visible, anyway, even with the blinds closed. I decide to leave them open for now. I'll close them once it's completely dark outside.

"Mom!" Rosemarie practically shouts. "Focus. You're driving us insane. Tell us, already!"

"Sorry," I say, shaking my head.

"Don't apologize," Hank says.

Silas eyes him, making it clear that their fledgling friendship will come to a swift end if he interferes with our family dynamic. I don't want any strife, so I speak up.

"Blackmail," I say. "Let's get back to that."

"Please," Rosemarie says again. "Who is blackmailing you? What do they want?'

I draw a big, deep breath. I hope what I'm about to say doesn't change the way they see me. "Your dad is right," I confirm. "It's money they're after."

Becca lifts a hand to her mouth. "My stars," she mutters.

"I guess it's pretty obvious that our interior design firm is doing well, and so are Silas' hotels," I continue. "We must look like easy targets."

Silas shakes his head and scoffs, but he looks confused. "Okay, sure," he concedes, "but what do they want?"

Here's where things get tricky for me. I'll need to tell my family nothing but the truth, yet I don't want them to know the whole story. I need time to figure things out on my own first. "Ten million dollars," I blurt.

"Ten million dollars?" Rosemarie asks, incredulous. "That's a lot of money. Do we have that much money?"

I nod. "We do."

Silas and I tend not to discuss money with our daughter. It's a touchy subject. Maybe that's because we both spent portions of our childhoods as poor as church mice. Most of our money conversations happen in bed at night, when it's dark outside and the world sleeps. Maybe, somewhere in the backs of our minds, we're afraid we'll lose it all if we get too comfortable and speak about it in the light of day. I must admit, there's an underlying terror that haunts me. No matter how much money I earn or how much we save, a part of me remains afraid that it will somehow cause trouble and then vanish into thin air. It doesn't make logical sense, I know. It doesn't have to.

"Son of a bitch," Hank says, mostly to himself. "That's fuck you money, right there."

Becca raises her brows, but nods. She knows how well our firm has done. She can't be too surprised.

I shrug nervously. "What can I say? Business has been good."

Rosemarie cocks her head to one side, as if she's doing mental math. "If we have ten million, that probably means we have even more, right?"

I look at Silas, unsure how much he wants to reveal. "That's right," he confirms. "Like your mother said, business has been good. Thanks to that and some smart investments, we're set nicely. You don't ever have to worry about money," he says as he reaches over and brushes a strand of hair from our daughter's cheek and tucks it behind her ear. "That isn't to say you don't have to work at something productive when you're an adult. You do. Everyone should. But you'll never have to worry."

The wheels in Rosemarie's head are turning fast. "Except when someone notices that I'm rich and tries to blackmail me like they're doing to Mom?"

"Oh, honey," I say. I don't want her to draw that conclusion. There's more going on here. "Don't think that."

"Make it make sense then," she says abruptly.

"I want to," I say. "Sometimes things don't make as much sense as we'd like."

Silas turns his attention back to me. "Who's doing this?"

I take another deep breath. "I'm not sure yet. Remember how the guy who broke into our house yesterday took my laptop?" I ask.

"Yeah?" Silas replies.

I hadn't told Silas about the man's reappearance when I'd asked him to bring Rosemarie and the dogs down. He hadn't mentioned the events of today. We both knew there would be time to discuss things later.

"Well, the same guy showed up at Moxie Tavern while Becca and I were having lunch there today," I explain. "It took me a few minutes to recognize him, but once I did, I knew for sure it was the same guy. Hank ran him off."

"Thank you, Hank," Silas says, then narrows his eyes as he looks back at me. "Did he follow you down from the North Shore?"

"I don't think so," I say. "At least, I didn't notice any cars following me. The Causeway is only two lanes in either direction. You'd think I would have noticed if I was being followed."

"True," Silas says. "He must have tracked your car."

"That's what I thought, too," I reply. "Which is why I left it in the city lot near the tavern. Hank called in a favor and had someone pick us up in the back alley. Then we transferred cars in the parking lot of the Voodoo Museum, just to be sure we made a clean break."

"And your phone?" Silas asks.

"I took the SIM card out and left it on Hank's desk at the tavern," I confirm.

Silas leans back in his chair and laces his fingers together behind his head. "Wow," he says.

"Yeah," I say.

"Thank you, Hank," Rosemarie adds, suddenly sounding wiser than her years. "For helping my mom."

I hate that my daughter feels responsible enough for me that she'd thank a man she just met. Am I that much of a liability? I push the thought aside.

"You're very welcome," Hank says. "It's nothing, really. I'm always ready to help your mom. She and I go way back. That's what old friends are for." He shoves a hand through his graying hair, and I can't help but think he looks like a proud papa. I wish his own daughter would give him half a chance.

"So, how does the blackmail come into play?" Silas asks. "Is that the guy who wants ten mill?"

"Sussy," Rosemarie mumbles, then makes a clicking sound.

"What's that?" Hank asks.

I don't even pretend to know what it means. "Sussy?" I ask, turning to face Rosemarie.

She rolls her eyes, though her attitude is directed more at me than at Hank. It seems she's willing to offer grace to anyone and everyone else. "Suspicious," she says. "Sussy or sus, for short."

"Got it," Hank says, winking at Silas.

I nod. "That's the guy. He wrote his demands on a bar napkin, then handed it to Kristin, Hank's employee. Kristin gave it to me after Hank tossed him out. She didn't realize anything unusual was going on. The guy folded the napkin a few times and asked her to pass it along. She said she thought maybe it was a business thing, or that he had a crush and was giving me his number."

"Yeah, right," Rosemarie says.

"Hey," I reply. "What makes that so hard to believe?"

"Because you're old, for one," she replies. "And look at the way you dress."

Her comments sting, as usual. "Damn," I say softly. My skin isn't feeling very thick right now. I'm out of sorts, given the situation at hand. "Rosemarie, you're hurting my feelings. Low-key."

Becca purses her lips and reaches for my hand across the table. "It's okay, Mer," she says softly. "I'd date you."

At that, we laugh. It's another much-needed break in the tension. Becca is proving good at lightening the mood.

"Thank you, my friend," I reply.

Instinctively, I turn my body away from my daughter. I believe she has a right to be here, and I love her, of course. I'm not sure I can handle her jabs right now. Silas glances at me, but doesn't get involved.

"Anyway," I continue, "the note said the thing about the ten million dollars."

"What's the blackmail?" Silas asks. "We're transparent people. Not to mention, we aren't criminals. What on earth could they be threatening you with?"

Here's the part I'm not ready to share. I chew my lip as I figure out how to deflect. I say the words slowly, my mind forming them carefully. "He says he will leak incriminating information that will affect our reputations … if that information becomes public knowledge."

That much is true, if indirectly. It's my mom whose reputation would be affected most. I wish I didn't feel like I had to protect her. I wish I didn't care about her at all. As much as I hate to admit it, I do care. And as difficult and infuriating as she is, she's my mom. The only parent I have left.

Silas isn't impressed. He drops his hands and leans forward in his chair again. "I'm not so sure. I call BS," he says. "What could he possibly leak that would affect our reputations? That sounds vague. Like a feeble attempt at blackmail, if you ask me."

My brows shoot up, but I force them back down. I know that this thing has teeth. I know what the man is referring to, and it's something I definitely don't want coming to light. "I don't know everything," I say. "Just bits and pieces." That much is also true.

"Who is this guy?" Silas asks. "Do you know what his motivation is, besides money? Why us? There are plenty of other wealthy folks he could target. There has to be some reason he picked us."

I know the answer to that question, too, but I don't

want to divulge it. "Maybe there is," I say. "I don't know him personally. I'd never seen him until today." All true.

"What do you think he wanted with your laptop?" Hank asks, innocently. I didn't fill him in on the backstory. It didn't seem right to tell Hank or Becca things that I didn't plan to tell my own husband. So, I didn't.

"I guess he wanted to look through my files," I reply. "He must have thought he'd find something in there that he could use."

"Is there anything there?" Becca asks. "Because you wanted to talk to me about something very serious at lunch, but we never got down to it. What were you going to say?"

Before I can answer her, the doorbell rings. A jolt of fear travels through me. I'm genuinely afraid of who might be out front. At the same time, though, I'm grateful to be saved from this conversation, even if only for a few minutes.

"Stay here," Silas says to the others. "I'll get it."

11

ROUNDABOUT

RUTHIE

Nashville

We remain silent as we ride. Rae steers the car around twists and turns, taking back roads from my home in Brentwood to the trendy 12South neighborhood in Nashville proper.

I'm not sure why she's driving this way or where she intends to take us. She didn't say anything more than that she thought we could all use some fresh air. My gut tells me this is a trial run. Rae and Dahlia want to see how well I hold up on a short, local trip. I'm already feeling weak and shaky, but I will myself to stay strong. I need them to believe that I can make it to New Orleans without a major incident.

Finally, I can't bear the silence any longer.

"Where are we going?" I ask as I grip the armrest beside me. I'm so unsteady that I need a handhold to stay upright. I realize that doesn't bode well for the trip south.

Rae smiles. Even in the low light, I can see the familiar

corners of her mouth turn upward. She's blessed with a cheerful, friendly face. "I thought we could all use some fresh air," she says.

"Fresh air, huh?" I ask. "You said that before. When did fresh air become such a high priority?"

Dahlia clears her throat in the backseat. "It's a nice night," she says.

I immediately feel bad. I must sound snippy. I don't intend to. "It *is* a nice night," I agree. "Forgive my tone. I guess I'm a little on edge. Mitch says my daughter is in danger, after all."

Your time is running out.

"No worries," Rae says.

"Seriously, though," I continue, "where are we headed? Aren't most places around here closed by now?"

"We could get ice cream," Rae says.

"After the dessert we already ate?" Dahlia asks. "No, ma'am. I don't think so. You'll have to roll me around like a giant bowling ball if I eat another bite."

"Same here," I say.

"Party poopers," Rae says with a laugh. "You two aren't any fun."

Dahlia reaches forward and smacks Rae playfully on the arm. "You hush," she says.

Rae pretends to be hurt, then laughs heartily.

I enjoy watching the two of them have a good time together. Seeing happy couples sometimes makes me sad because I miss Pete so much. Rae and Dahlia make me appreciate the glory of love, though. They make me smile because I had the great honor of experiencing a love like theirs, once upon a time. Truth be told, the only part of dying that I'm looking forward to is the chance to see my Pete once again. He had better be waiting for me when I reach those pearly gates.

As we turn onto 12th Avenue South, the main drag in the local hotspot, Rae drives slowly and rolls the windows down. "A restaurant client of mine had their grand opening celebration recently. You ladies want to take a look in person?" she asks.

"Absolutely," Dahlia replies.

"Sure!" I say, enthusiastically. "As long as we can chat about my predicament at some point this evening." I love interior design and am thrilled with the prospect of seeing what Rae is doing for her clients. "What's the name of the restaurant?"

"It's a cereal bar," Rae explains as she makes a right on Caruthers Avenue and parks on the side of the street in front of a freshly painted black and white house that's been converted for commercial use. "It's called Wanna Spoon Cereal Bar. The sign's right there on the front of the building, beneath the goose neck lanterns."

"A cereal bar?" I ask with a laugh. "If that isn't Nashville, I don't know what is. We're almost too trendy for our own good. I love it."

"That's right," Rae replies. "Cereal, coffee, and a space out back for events. Customers are digging it."

Dahlia smiles proudly from the backseat. I get the idea she's been here before.

"You designed this?" I ask as I gaze out the open window.

"Not this building," Rae replies, "but I'm working on a new concept for the owners. Well, after I'm finished with the guitar-themed monstrosity in the Gulch, that is. I've been here a few times to meet with them and loved the vibe. We could go sit out back for a bit, if you like. The owners won't mind. Shop's closed for the day, anyway. Cereal tends to be more of a morning thing for the early risers."

"Okay," I say. "Let's go look."

Energized by the idea of touring the cereal bar, I open my car door and lean forward. A white fence made with pickets in the shape of spoons greets me. Dahlia hops out of the backseat and rushes to my aid, giving me a hand as I climb out of the car. Rae positions herself on my other side and the two of them walk me in.

"You feeling strong enough, Ruthie?" Dahlia asks.

I nod. "I'm good." I hope I'm not overselling it. My legs are awfully shaky.

A wide concrete path leads to a handful of wide wooden stairs. I glance to our left and notice a ramp option, but decide to try the stairs. With Rae and Dahlia's help, I make it to the porch on top. We pass a metal bistro set and a large black and white striped patio umbrella.

"Isn't it charming?" Dahlia asks, a smile spreading across her face. I nod. "Wait until you see inside."

"So, you've been here before?" I ask.

"A time or two," she replies. "I like to meet Rae's clients whenever I can. I'm her biggest fan. Besides, we live nearby."

I'd forgotten that part, actually. Dahlia has spent so much time at my house lately that I practically think of her as living there with me. "Oh, yeah, you do," I say.

"Your condo is in Hillsboro Village. I know that. Silly me." She knows what I mean.

"Come on," Rae says. "The door is unlocked. A single employee—a part time bookkeeper—occupies an office in the back this time of night, but we won't bother her."

We continue through the inside of the building, walking arm in arm. Rae points out a rope swing hung near the front, accented by a decorative wall covered in fruity cereal pieces. We walk around the cereal bar and make our way to the backyard, where more tables are shaded by black and white striped umbrellas. Brightly colored Adirondack chairs fill the open spaces, and a cow statue sits against a black and white wooden fence. String lights make the space uber cozy.

"Have a seat," Rae says, gesturing to a bright blue chair.

"I'd love to," I say, remembering the dinner from earlier in the evening and how sweetly Rae and Dahlia doted on me. They help me get comfortable.

"What do you think of the place?" Rae asks as she sits on a bench nearby. Dahlia settles beside her, then they join hands.

"It's quirky and cute. Definitely unique," I reply. "You have me curious about the new concept. Can you talk about it yet?"

Rae shrugs. "Oh, sure. I can talk about it with you. Just don't go telling a reporter from the Nashville Scene or anything."

I laugh, then pretend to zip my lips. "Under lock and key," I say. "I'm not exactly talking to many reporters these days."

"Good, then. It's a build-your-own sandwich place," Rae begins, "kind of like Which Wich, only you actually make your own sandwich instead of just choosing the ingredients and letting a kid in the back put everything together."

"Huh," I say. "Interesting. Couldn't you make your own sandwich at home?"

"Well, yeah, you could," Rae says, "but it probably wouldn't be as good. We will offer premium ingredients—gourmet breads, meats, cheeses, from-scratch sauces, and locally-sourced vegetables. Think of it like one big, scrumptious sandwich board with an assortment of fillings. We're still toying around with names, but we will probably end up describing the concept as a sandwich bar."

"We?" I ask, leaning back in my chair and enjoying the warm night air on my skin. "I thought you were the interior designer. How did you get involved with choosing a name and concept title, too?"

Rae and Dahlia look at each other contentedly. "I told you, she's sharp," Dahlia says to her girlfriend. "You have to tell her everything now."

"Please do," I implore. A random pain moves through my chest, but I ignore it. Random pains are par for the course these days.

"Good catch, Ruthie," Rae says, turning her attention back to me. "I'm going in on this one as a co-owner. I'm ready to get my feet wet in the world of small business ownership. I hope you'll come to eat at the new place when it opens." She grins, and pride oozes from every pore.

My heart surges with simultaneous feelings of excitement and sadness. I'm so proud of Rae and so pleased for her. Yet I know there's no possible way I'll live long enough to see her sandwich bar open. Not a chance. Like she said, she has to finish designing the hotel in the Gulch first. It will probably take a year or longer to see the new sandwich place come to life. With potential permitting delays happening in Davidson County and the nationwide shortage of building materials, the timeline could easily stretch to two or more years. I'll be nothing but a faint memory by then.

Your time is running out.

The ladies stare silently, waiting for my response.

I'm keenly aware of the absence of Rae's own mother at this moment. From everything Rae has told me, the bigoted woman won't take her daughter's calls, let alone share in this major life milestone. The pressure is on me to fill some of that void. I want to fill it. I wish I could. It would mean a lot to us both.

If only my broken heart could find a way to heal. I have so much to live for. Maybe I didn't realize just how much. Maybe if I had, my heart wouldn't have failed me.

"That's … wonderful," I stammer. "I'm happy for you."

"You don't sound too happy, Ruthie," Rae says. "What's going on?"

Tears threaten to spring from my eyes, despite my best efforts to maintain my composure. "I can't help but think about how I'm letting you down," I say. "You and everyone else."

Rae stands, then moves a chair close to mine and sits.

"Nonsense," she says as she gently pats my forearm. "You're the best, my dear. You aren't letting me down. I'm so proud to share my big news with you tonight. You're only the second person I've told—after Dahlia."

With that, I'm definitely crying. I sob, tears streaming down my cheeks. I feel my heart thump and thud in my chest in response to my heightened emotion. It feels dangerous. Precarious. "That's so kind of you," I mumble. "So special."

"Then why the tears?"

"You know why," I say, my face knotting up even tighter.

Rae leans back a bit, allowing me room to grieve. Her touch is gentle. Her eyes, forgiving. "How about you tell me? It's good to let your feelings out."

Dahlia nods, then pulls up a third chair. "She's right, my dear, Ruthie. Let those tears flow. This is a safe space."

I cry for what feels like hours. Beneath the string lights and the moonlight, I sputter and I heave, the weight of my sadness lightened by the love of true friends who are kind enough to simply be with me. They're quiet, following my lead. When I'm ready, I dry my eyes and I speak.

"I'm losing so much," I say softly. "I won't be here when your sandwich bar opens."

"Maybe not, but I bet you'll be here in spirit," Rae replies compassionately. She speaks the truth with a loving kindness. "You haven't even heard the best part."

I sit straighter in my chair, eager for more good news, even if it still makes me sad. "What's the best part?" I ask.

Rae lifts one shoulder playfully, becoming more animated. "I have to run it by my business partners, but

I'd like to call the place Ruthie's. With your blessing, of course."

My eyes widen and my jaw drops. "Really?" I ask. I'm awed.

"Yeah, absolutely," Rae replies. "Do you remember the first time we met?"

It takes me a minute, but then it all comes flooding back. "I do," I say. "You came to lunch at my house. With Dahlia. It was springtime, and we ate on the back patio near the garden. The dogwoods were blooming, and the hills in the distance looked downright heavenly, all gussied up for the growing season."

"That's right," Rae confirms as Dahlia smiles broadly. "You made sandwiches. Amazing, gourmet sandwiches. I swear, I could taste the love."

I gasp, remembering. It was a few years ago now, back before I was sick. Life was full of promise then. Full of possibility. Another wave of emotion overtakes me. I cover my mouth with one hand and grasp Rae's shoulder with the other. "That's right," I say. "I made *sandwiches*. Aww, Rae, you're making this old woman happy. How special."

Rae is a woman who stays pretty even keel, but this is getting to her. She wipes a tear from her eye. "I'm glad you like it," she says. "I thought I'd decorate the place like your house. The kitchen and patio being prominent."

"That sounds lovely," I say as Dahlia beams.

"As long as you don't mind me imitating your style," Rae adds.

"Are you kidding me? It would be an honor for you to imitate my style," I reply. "One of the biggest honors of my life. I don't know how to thank you, Rae. Words don't feel like enough."

She leans over and hugs my neck tenderly. When she pulls away, she smiles. "Ruthie, your friendship and your faith in me has given me the confidence I needed to learn and grow. Since I didn't get it from my own mom—" She chokes back tears.

"It's been my true pleasure," I say. "Your friendship and admiration has given me great comfort. Since I didn't get it from my own daughter." Now it's my turn to sob once more. The emotion is overwhelming. In a good way.

"I guess we're a good group," Dahlia says. "A good team."

"I guess we are," I reply. "It's such an awful shame I won't be around longer. There's so much we could do together. And if I could reunite with Meredith and get to know my granddaughter … wouldn't life be glorious?"

"It sure would," Rae agrees. "But hey, we'll take what time we can get. It's a beautiful night, we're here together, and you aren't out of time just yet, Ms. Flores."

"Amen to that," Dahlia adds.

We smile, basking in the warmth of each other's company. My body is getting cold, though. The temperature has dropped since we first arrived. A chill runs through me. Always attuned to my needs, the ladies notice.

"If it gets cold out here, I have a blanket in the car," Dahlia says. "Want me to run and get it?"

"You're too good to me," I say. "If you don't mind grabbing it, that would be great. It's getting chilly. At least, it is for my old, frail bones." Then I think things through.

"Wait, when did you have time to put a blanket in the car? Did you plan this? I thought we were going for a spur of the moment drive, then visiting this place on a whim. Was there more to it?"

They glance at each other. "Easy on the conspiracy theories," Rae says with a chuckle. "We put the blanket in the car while you were sleeping. We had plenty of time." She chuckles.

"Is that all?" I ask, sensing more.

Dahlia finishes her girlfriend's thought while wearing a mischievous grin. "We put the blanket in the car … along with some other things we thought you'd need during our road trip to New Orleans."

My eyes light up. I can hardly believe what I just heard. They're actually doing it. "Are you serious right now?" I ask. "You'll take me down there?"

"If you still want to go," Rae says. "Then yes, we will. I have some vacation time to use and Dahlia, well, as you know, she hasn't been working much lately."

"She works for me, and I intend to keep paying her," I say. Dahlia waves a hand in the air, dismissing that topic. "But hell yes," I continue, "I most definitely want to go! I didn't want to be presumptuous, but I hoped you'd ask."

"Then it's settled," Dahlia says, turning and planting a kiss on Rae's lips. She seems pleased.

"When do we leave?" I ask, my voice teeming with excitement.

"How does tomorrow morning sound?" Rae asks. "Nurse Anne comes at eight. I figured we could let her check you out and maybe get a few travel tips, then we can leave by ten."

"Perfect!" I say. "I'll need to pack."

"It's already done," Dahlia says proudly. "I'm sure you'll want to take a look for yourself to make sure we didn't forget anything, but we did the bulk of it."

"I'm speechless," I say.

"Good," Dahlia replies. "We know how important this is to you, my dear. We all know the risks, but taking you to see your daughter and meet your granddaughter seems worth it. We're glad to be a part of the journey."

"I'm sure it will be a trip to remember," Rae adds.

I wipe my damp eyes, feeling tired but exhilarated. "Will we take two days to drive down?" I ask.

"At least," Rae says. "We'll see how you hold up. The drive is about nine total hours, not counting stops or traffic delays. It might be wise to break the ride into three days."

I sigh. "I hope we can do it in two. I hate to sound impatient, but … you know."

Your time is running out.

"We know," Rae replies. "Like my dad used to say, though, slow is smooth and smooth is fast. Better to take it easy and avoid problems that will do nothing but slow us down further."

I smile. "I've never heard you mention your dad like that before," I say.

"Yeah, well, don't read too much into it. He taught me a few things, but that doesn't mean I want him in my life. Not after the way he handled my coming out."

"Understood," I confirm, then I steer the conversation back to our travel plans. It's what I most want to talk about, anyway, and I don't want Rae to feel like I'm prying. "So, where will we stay in New Orleans? Like I said, I have plenty of money to pay for anything we may need."

"That's generous of you," Dahlia says.

"It is," Rae agrees.

"You two are the generous ones, taking me down there —and in my condition, no less. The least I can do is cover our costs."

They look at each other, then Rae nods. "Okay, then. We'll take you up on that. We appreciate it."

We don't talk about money much, but I know Rae and Dahlia essentially live paycheck to paycheck with little savings. They're young, still paying off student loans, and they don't come from family money. I was in their shoes once. It gives me pleasure to make things easier for them. And truly, I owe them everything for taking me to my daughter and granddaughter. No question.

"You're welcome," I say. "I appreciate you two. I could never thank you enough."

Dahlia smiles. "It's all good, my dear." She pauses briefly, then launches right into talk of trip logistics. I can hardly wait. "I think we should stay on the North Shore. Somewhere near Meredith's house, but not too close. We don't want to freak her out."

"Agreed," I say. "We need to approach Meredith nice and easy. Have you done any research on the area yet? I haven't been to New Orleans in ages, and I've only driven through the North Shore once. I'm sure it's totally different now."

"As a matter of fact, I did do a little research," Dahlia replies. Of course, she did. That's my girl. "Mitch says Meredith lives in Mandeville, right on the lake. I think we should stay in nearby Covington. It's very close, but provides some breathing room. I found a couple of cute vacation rental homes we could stay in."

I nod enthusiastically. "Okay."

"Renting a home seems like the smart play," Rae adds. "It will be easier for us to take care of you there. Plus, we'll all have more privacy in our own bedrooms." Dahlia blushes, but Rae continues without acknowledging her embarrassment. "A house is best for cooking, that's for sure. A full kitchen will allow us to make meals instead of having to get takeout every day. We want to be sure you're eating nutritious food that will help you to keep your strength."

"You've thought of everything," I say.

"Maybe not everything, but we've tried to cover the basics," Rae replies. "I'll do some remote work on my laptop when there's time. Dahlia will care for you while I work, as usual. I took the liberty of ordering some medical supplies from a company down there. A wheelchair, hospital bed, shower chair, and all the extras we thought you might need will be at the rental home when we arrive. I just need to give them an address."

"Brilliant!" I say, feeling like this might actually work. "Let's book the house. Which one do you recommend?"

I get out my credit card as Rae pulls up the listings on her phone. She shows me three properties, but one stands out above the others. It's a three bedroom bungalow in the historic district that has been completely renovated. A plaque beside the front door from the Covington Heritage Foundation indicates the historic home status, circa 1898.

"That's the one," Dahlia says.

"It's perfect," I say, and I mean it. "If I don't make it home—"

"Stop it," Dahlia says, interrupting. She turns to face me with the most serious expression on her face. "Don't talk like that, Ruthie."

I shrug. Rae eyes me. She's the realist. She raises a hand in Dahlia's direction, telling her to let me speak.

"All I'm saying is that if I should die down there, in that home, it looks like a good place," I say. "That's all. It suits me."

Rae nods, then takes my card and enters the details to confirm the reservation.

"How long are you reserving it for?" I ask as she types furiously on her phone.

"Let's do a month," Rae says. "It's cheaper that way, and I bet you'll need more time than you think."

"Really?" I ask. "That long? I don't know if I'll be alive in a month. I realize that sounds morbid, but it's the God's honest truth."

"Let's assume you will be," Rae says. "Besides, we don't want to have to move to a new location before we're ready. Once we get settled, I want to stay put."

"A lot can happen in a month," Dahlia says softly.

I chew my lip as I consider the implications. "That's true," I say. "Rae, are you sure you can be away from work for that long? Do you have that much vacation time saved up?"

She nods assuringly. "I do. I promise. Don't worry about that. Like I said, I'll do a little work when I can. If not for the hotel, I'll work on plans for the sandwich bar concept. The time away will actually be to my advantage, because it will allow me to get a jump on my own endeavors. So, you're helping me out, Ruthie."

I grab Rae's hand and squeeze it. I'm overwhelmed with gratitude. I hardly know what to say or how to act. Unfortunately, I'm getting tired and can tell that I won't be able to stay upright much longer. I'll need to lean heavily on Rae and Dahlia if I'm to make this trip a success. We haven't even talked about a plan to get Meredith to talk to me. To let me help her out of the danger Mitch says she's in. Magdalena and the information she gathers will be a key factor. I need to get back in touch with her right away.

"I know what you're thinking," Dahlia says when I'm quiet for a few moments.

"Yeah?" I ask. "What's that?"

"You're cold, and you're already tired," she guesses, correctly. "You're wondering how you'll make it to New Orleans."

I nod. "I am exhausted. I hate it. I can't help myself. There's more to discuss. I need to come up with more detailed plans—for Southern Charm Society. I have to tell you about what I've done so far. I have to keep strategizing. To keep going. To find a way to help my daughter."

"We've got you," Dahlia says. "You do what you can when you can, and we'll take care of the rest."

"That's right," Rae confirms. "You can count on us for the heavy lifting."

I chuckle. "You might have to literally lift me, so heavy lifting is probably an understatement."

"We've got you," Rae reiterates. "Don't you worry

about a thing. There will be plenty of time to talk and strategize on the ride down."

I nod and breathe a sigh of relief. "Okay, you miracle workers, you. We'll tackle more tomorrow. This has been an evening I'll never, ever forget. Not even when I'm gone from this body and this life. This memory will stay with me. I guarantee it."

"Good, my dear," Dahlia coos.

"Now," I say, "please help me out of this chair and back into the car. My warm bed is calling my name."

PART III

BURIED

12

FAST AND SLOW

MEREDITH

New Orleans

"**Y**ou don't have to handle this alone," Hank says to Silas as they both push up from the dining table. "I'll go with you to get the door."

"That won't be necessary," Silas says, although I detect a tone of uncertainty in his voice.

The dogs are barking like crazy. I can barely hear over their loud woofs. I grab my husband's arm then pull his ear toward me. "Let him help," I say.

"I can protect my family," he replies, "all on my own."

His feelings sound hurt. I didn't mean to imply anything insulting. "You certainly can," I say. "But what's the harm? You can trust Hank. I promise."

Hank pauses, waiting for Silas' okay. I don't think he heard what I said, but he gets the gist. "I don't mean to intrude," he says earnestly. "I only want to do what I can to help out. That's all. I like to feel useful."

That, Silas understands. He nods quickly, then

motions for Hank to follow. "Stay put," he says to the rest of us. He makes direct eye contact with Rosemarie to reassure her.

"Okay, Daddy," she says. "Hurry up. Whoever it is needs to go away."

I grab Calliope's collar and hold her close against my leg. We don't want a repeat of this morning's jaunt around the neighborhood. We aren't on the North Shore anymore. On these streets, in Central City, the pup is liable to get hit in traffic. No one stops the hustle and bustle for a wandering dog in these parts. "Calliope, *stay*," I command. I let Alphie and Sara continue to bark protectively. Maybe it will send a message that's enough to deter anyone who might want to cause trouble.

My pulse quickens as Silas and Hank approach the door. Taking care to avoid being seen through the two large windows on the front of the house, Silas slides the wooden lever out of the way and looks through the keyhole. Within seconds, he jerks his head back, then motions for Hank to lean in. Hank peers through the keyhole, then recoils with much the same expression on his face.

"What do you see?" Becca asks. She's staying in her seat, but she's nervous. Her muscles are tense. She's wringing her hands. It's a distance from where we are to the front door, but it's all open space. Sounds carry.

"I don't see anything," Silas says. "Do you?" he asks Hank.

"No one's in view," Hank replies, then he reaches over to close the blinds. "Something isn't right."

I suddenly feel like we're in a real-life horror movie,

waiting for the jump scare. It's almost completely dark outside now. I can't help but wonder where the person who rang our bell is hiding. "What do you mean you don't see anyone?" I ask. "The person didn't just vanish into thin air. They have to be out there somewhere."

"Mommy's right," Rosemarie says. Mommy again. My heart flutters.

Buoyed by her vote of confidence, I decide to get more involved. "I'll check out back," I say, standing.

"Whoa, wait, please," Silas says, raising his hands in the air.

"Just a second, now, Meredith," Hank echoes.

The way they're reacting, you'd think I just said I was going to throw myself to the wolves. Or the sharks. "I'm a big girl," I say. "I won't do anything stupid. I only want to check out back. I can even keep the glass door latched, if it makes you feel any better. I'll just look."

"Don't," Silas says, more sternly than I'd expect from him. "Please."

I release Calliope's collar and cross my arms over my chest. I'm not sure what to do. Sensing my hesitation, Becca weighs in.

"I think what Silas and Hank are trying to accomplish is to keep you out of sight," she explains. "After all, you're the one being targeted, for reasons we don't yet understand. It seems wise to let the guys handle this. I would, if I were you. Keep a low profile. You know?"

I exhale sharply, then plop back down onto my chair. "Fine," I say, gesturing toward the door. "Do your thing, guys. Save the day, and all that. Fuck!" I raise a hand to stop Rosemarie before she mentions my language, but it isn't necessary. She's too preoccupied to call me out.

Looking relieved, Silas and Hank resume their investigation of the mysterious doorbell ringer. They huddle up at the entryway as if they're on a football team waiting for a coach to tell them the next play. Only there's no coach, and no clear play to follow. None of us have been in a situation like this before. At least, not as far as I know.

"Should we go out onto the porch?" Hank asks.

"Oh, so it's safe for you to go?" I mutter. "Figures." No one gives me more than a passing glance.

"I'm not sure," Silas says to Hank. "Yesterday morning, at our house in Mandeville, the guy who broke in rang the doorbell first. He acted like a salesman and tried to get me off guard. Before I knew it, he was racing around to the side of the house and smashing through a glass door."

"You think this is the same?"

"Maybe. My gut tells me it isn't random or accidental, for what it's worth," Silas explains. "Especially given Meredith's … issue."

I can tell Silas wishes I'd tell him more about the blackmail. I realize that's a big word to throw around without a thorough and detailed story to back it up. My husband knows me well enough to know I'm holding something back. Most likely, they all do. I appreciate the fact that they're giving me a little space. It's exactly what I need until I can figure things out.

Hank shifts his weight. "I swear, man, we took precautions when getting the ladies here from my tavern.

I'd be awfully surprised if the guy I tossed out found a way to follow us. He didn't seem like he had it in him. If he did manage to follow us, well, then I'd be very concerned for our safety right now. That would be professional level. Know what I mean?"

Silas shoves a hand through his short hair and begins to pace in a tight circle. "You raise a good point," he says.

The dogs have stopped barking, but they remain on high alert. They're watching us like hawks, looking from one of us to the next for any clue as to what they should do.

Becca leans forward, covering both eyes with her hands. "I don't like this," she says. "We should call the police."

"No police!" I blurt. They all look at me, perplexed by my fervor. All except Hank, that is. He seems to have my back. Maybe. "I told you," I try again, my voice measured. "I don't want to involve the police, if we can help it."

Becca looks up. "Mer, what aren't you telling us? This doesn't make sense. It's creeping me out. Some guy is, apparently, after you. It seems to me like we need the police."

I shake my head. "No police. I have my reasons. Trust me. Okay? It's about something that happened a long time ago. The day my dad died. *How* my dad died."

Before they can respond, six loud knocks sound in rapid succession from the back of the house. I stiffen. There's someone out back, on the patio. No question about it. The dogs launch into more furious barking. We let them. No one dares tell the pups to quiet down now.

Within seconds, we hear another series of forceful knocks. This time they're coming from the front door, again. We freeze, unsure about what to do. Just when we think things can't get any worse, a third set of knocks sounds from the side door, next to the narrow driveway.

"They have us surrounded," Silas says in disbelief. "That can't be good."

We're stunned, but Hank springs into action. "Is there a landline here?" he asks.

I nod. "Yes."

"Where's the phone?"

"No police," I say again, foolishly. Although, I'm starting to doubt my own stance.

"Meredith, enough," Silas says firmly. He glances at our daughter then back at me.

It isn't like him to tell me what to do. Our marriage is a true partnership. I know he respects me as a strong, independent woman. Which makes me afraid now. My husband must think the danger we're in is very real.

"There's a phone on the console table in the living room," I explain. "At the end of the sofa, near the front window. Be careful."

The blinds may be closed, but anyone watching from out front will see Hank's silhouette if he moves around in the space. I'm scared for him. My heart swells with concern and protectiveness for the man. He took care of me when I was young and dumb. I don't want to see anything bad happen to him.

Hank nods, then—without words—he drops to the floor and begins to crawl toward the phone. He moves swiftly, surprising us with impressive speed and agility for a man his age. When he reaches the console table, he lifts one hand to pick up the receiver. He brings it to his ear, then scowls. He pauses a moment before saying the words that will strike fear in us all. "It's dead," he announces grimly.

"It's *what?*" Becca says, her voice rising.

"No dial tone," Hank clarifies. "I don't mean to alarm you folks, but someone must have cut the line. That's the only explanation, unless the phone company is doing work in the area. Landlines are fairly reliable. The line *shouldn't* be dead." He lowers his brow. "If we decide it's safe to go out, I suppose we could check with your neighbors to see if their phones are working. That doesn't seem—"

Insistent knocks sound again from all three doors, interrupting Hank. The knocks are coordinated this time. They sound like a perfectly synchronized chorus, accompanied by the protective woofing of our dogs. Alphie's hackles are raised high on his neck and back. I don't think I've ever seen him so upset. It's terrifying.

Rosemarie leaps toward me and wraps her arms around my waist. "Mommy, I'm scared. Even more scared than yesterday. It sounds like there are a lot of bad guys out there. And the smoking man—*Mitch*—isn't here to help Daddy chase them."

"I know," I whisper as I smooth her hair and pull her against me.

I can't tell her that everything will be all right because I'm not sure it will.

I'm surprised Rosemarie mentioned Mitch. Honestly, I wouldn't mind seeing his face right about now. I suspect we will need all the help we can get. He was brave yesterday. My dad would have been proud of his old friend. I consider calling Uncle Mitch, although I'm not confident I can find his number. It would probably take some digging to locate.

"Check your mobile phones," Hank says as he crawls back near Silas and stands.

We all pull phones out of our pockets and press various buttons on the screens.

"I don't seem to have a signal," Becca says. "That's weird … and frightening."

"Me neither," Silas says. "No bars. Wifi isn't working."

Hank looks at Rosemarie and me. We shake our heads. "Nothing for me," he confirms. "They must have a jammer."

Rosemarie lets out a squeaky noise that sounds like it belongs to a baby animal. "What's a jammer?" she asks.

"Aren't those illegal?" Becca asks.

"Yes, but that doesn't matter right now. No time to explain," Hank says, eyeing Silas.

I'm slightly irritated that my old friend is brushing us off. I get it, though. Time is of the essence.

Silas tenses even tighter. "What's the range on those things?" he asks.

Hank shrugs. "I'm no expert, but from what I understand, it isn't far. Twenty-five or thirty feet." He raises a hand to his chin, as if thinking things through. Or maybe he's thinking that we're in serious trouble.

Becca shudders. "Are you telling me that someone is standing thirty feet or less from us with a device that's blocking our phone signals?"

Hank nods, his lips pursed. He's sorry to be the bearer of bad news. "That'd be my guess," he says.

Rosemarie's face is contorted. She looks so innocent, yet suddenly so worldly and mature at the same time. A week ago, her biggest concern was a mean girl in her dance class. Now she's scared—and rightfully so—for her physical safety. "We can't call the police for help?" she asks. "Not even if Mommy wants to?" She looks up at me. "You've changed your mind, right, Mommy? You want to call the police now, *right?*" She nods slowly, urging me to agree.

I waffle, wondering if I'm doing the right thing. But it doesn't matter, anyway, because the phones don't work. "The phones are all dead, honey," I say. "We're going to have to deal with this on our own."

"Shit, shit, shit," Becca says. She's breathing hard now, like she might be having a panic attack. Her alarm isn't helping Rosemarie, who pulls her knees up to her chest and begins to rock back and forth.

"Look," Hank says, "we're sitting ducks here. We can talk about things later. We need to take action to protect ourselves and fortify the place as best we can."

Silas nods forcefully, building his resolve. "You're right." He points to Rosemarie, Becca, and me. "Go into the back bathroom, the one behind the guest room that has the laundry room attached. There's a small opening for attic access in there, above the washer. Stay in that bathroom with the door locked and don't come out until we tell you it's safe. If we don't arrive to give the all clear within twenty minutes or if you hear anyone closing in, you climb into the attic and hide there. Take something you can use as a weapon—the big flashlight under the kitchen sink will work. Do you understand?"

I'm stunned. I'm also torn. I'm not inclined to hide like a coward. I'm a strong, capable woman. I want to help Hank and Silas. My husband can tell what I'm thinking, and he interrupts my internal debate.

"Meredith, this isn't the time for keeping up with the boys. As much as I love and admire you, you don't have the physical strength to fight with intruders as front-line defense. I need you to keep our daughter safe. Right now, that means you hide her. Do you understand?" he says.

Hank looks on, concerned..

I freeze. I can't believe this is happening. I don't *want* this to be happening. I feel like a little girl who just wants her daddy to burst in and save the day, making everything all right. Only my daddy died twenty years ago. There's no way he can save me. And my mom … yeah, well, she's practically useless. I'm not sure she'd even care that my family and I are in danger, let alone do anything about it, if she did know.

Silas is right. I have a kid of my own to protect. That has to be my focus now. Those of us in this house are on our own. Right here. Right now. We don't know the intentions of the people outside. The actions we take—or don't take—could mean the difference between living and dying today.

Rosemarie notices that I'm holding my breath and she slaps me on the back, hard. "Breathe, Mommy! Answer Daddy."

Her big brown eyes snap me out of it. "Okay, yes, I

understand," I say, jumping to my feet. "Find objects we can take with us. Quickly!"

"Should we take the dogs?" Rosemarie asks. "I don't want them to get loose."

"They'll bark," Becca says as she stands on shaky legs that seem like they might give out on her at any minute. "They'll give us away."

Silas and I look at each other. I'm with the program now, thinking strategically about what we can and should do. "If they get inside, the intruders will know soon, anyway," I say. "This house isn't big enough to hide anywhere for long. Maybe the dogs will fight for us, if it comes down to that. And if it doesn't, then we keep them from getting out. I say we take them with us. Into the bathroom."

Silas nods his agreement. "Go!" he says. "If you can, drag something in front of the door. The washer or dryer, if you can manage it."

Rosemarie, Becca, and I hurry into the bathroom, picking up random heavy objects along the way. We tell the dogs to follow, and they do, reluctantly. They seem grateful for the direction. As we go, I hear Hank and Silas talking in low tones near the front of the house. I can barely hear them, but I get the gist.

Hank wants to know if we have firearms here and where they're stored. Silas tells him that we're a gun-free family. That we've never needed a gun before. That we haven't felt comfortable owning one given the potential for accidents, especially with kids around. That we'd never forgive ourselves if Rosemarie and her friends got ahold of the gun and someone got hurt.

That's all true, but in hindsight, it seems foolish. How are we supposed to protect ourselves now? My dad taught me how to use a rifle. We used to shoot at targets on my parents' property in the hills of Tennessee. He said he wanted me to know my way around a weapon, just in case. I sure wish I had one at my disposal.

Hank mumbles something, then I hear the distinctive sound of a gun being locked and loaded. "Thank God," I say, without looking back.

I close the bathroom door behind me with a sigh of relief. I feel better knowing that Hank has a weapon. If we make it out of here alive, I plan to go get one myself.

Inside the bathroom, Becca helps me move the washer in front of the door. When it's in place, we sit down on the floor, and we wait.

13

SOUTHBOUND

RUTHIE

Nashville

"Good morning, sunshine," Dahlia says as she opens the shades in my room. Bright light fills the space greedily, as if it's been eagerly waiting for the chance. "Time to get up and at 'em. We have a big day ahead."

I stretch, rubbing my weary eyes. I've been too amped to sleep much. "Already?" I ask. "I don't think I fell into a deep sleep until an hour or so ago."

Dahlia's dressed in casual clothes today—a pastel pink wrap on top of black yoga pants and off-white running shoes. It's unusual to see her without her trademark skirts and heels. "Yes, already," she says as she moves a stack of my clothes from a dresser to the foot of my bed. "Come now. Anne will be here in a half hour to examine you before we hit the road. We need to get you cleaned up and dressed. Plus, I want to get your bedding through the wash before we go."

I reach down and feel the bed beneath me. As usual, it's soaked. I chuckle thinking about how nasty these wet sheets would be if we left them here to fester for a month while we're away. "Good idea," I say. "Thank you."

"Your spirits are good this morning," Dahlia says. "No complaining about your incontinence or talk of feeling guilty because I have to do the wash?"

I smile at her. "We're still leaving for New Orleans today, aren't we?" I ask.

She nods cheerfully. "We are. Rae is packing the van now."

"The van?" I ask. "I don't remember any of us owning a van. Is my memory failing me now, too? As if a bad heart isn't enough."

She shrugs playfully. "We might have purchased a van for the occasion."

I prop up on one elbow. "You *what?* I don't want to put you two out. You should have asked me and I could have taken care—"

"Relax," she says, waving a hand my way. "Rae's been eyeing minivans for a while. She figures it will be easy to carry her design stuff in the back. You know how much miscellaneous junk us designers end up hauling around— color wheels, flooring samples, schematics. That doesn't even count the furniture and window treatments we inevitably end up transporting at the last minute. The fact that it will be easier for you to get into and out of the van is a bonus. Consider it serendipitous timing."

"You don't think it will look like an uncool mom van?" I ask.

I immediately wish I hadn't mentioned the word mom,

though. I've never talked to Dahlia and Rae about the prospect of marriage, let alone kids. I don't want to pry. That said, I suppose I am a little curious. They'd make great parents, when they're ready. If they choose to have children.

Dahlia laughs. "When have you known Rae to care what other people think of her?" she asks. "That woman is blessed with rock-solid self esteem. It's admirable."

"Except when it comes to her parents, perhaps," I muse as I work my way into a sitting position. Dahlia bristles. "I'm sorry," I say quickly. "Forget about that. Where are my manners this morning?"

I've noticed myself losing whatever filter I once had. Everything feels too urgent now. Too pressing. I can't bring myself to care as much about social faux pas as I used to. I'd rather say what's on my mind. I don't have the luxury of time to waste. That said, though, I don't want to hurt feelings either.

Dahlia hesitates, and I'm unsure whether she's mad at me. "We'll let that topic rest for now," she says.

I nod my agreement. "Yes, sorry. What model of minivan? And where did Rae get it?"

Dahlia smiles again, happy with the lighter topic. "It's a—"

Rae walks into the bedroom and finishes the sentence for her. "A Chrysler Pacifica," she says. "A brand-spankin' new hybrid, top-of-the-line Pinnacle Model in Fathom Blue. It's the nicest vehicle I've ever purchased." She beams, the pride from a job well done written all over her face.

Rae is a diligent, hard worker who is seeing the fruits

of her labor. She deserves this. She should be proud.

"Well, then," I say. "My hearty congratulations!"

Rae grabs Dahlia's hand and gives it a squeeze, then pats me on the shoulder with the other. "I picked it up last night, after you went to bed, Ruthie. You'll be the first to ride in it, along with Dahlia, of course."

I'm pleased to hear that I only slept for one night. *Thank God*. I was afraid I'd lose too much time.

"Can't wait," I reply. "Maybe along the way, I can help you come up with a name for the new ride."

I own a Lexus SUV that might be more comfortable, but I don't mention it. Rae is proud and she's doing a very nice thing for me. I'll appreciate every single kind gesture I can get.

"A name for my van?" Rae asks as she shoves both hands into the pockets of her jeans and rocks onto her toes. I nod. "She's already named."

"Do tell!" I exclaim.

"I named her Indie," Rae explains. "Because an independent spirit is so important to me—independence in my work life as I move toward entrepreneurship, independence in my personal style and design style as I grow and evolve." She pauses and looks contemplative before continuing. "Independence from my parents."

I raise my brows. "I see." I look at Dahlia to find out if she plans to share my comment about Rae's self esteem. She doesn't make eye contact, so I'll assume she intends to keep quiet. I wait for a few beats, then decide to change the subject and move on. "Indie sounds lovely. What time do we leave?"

I can tell by the brightness outside that it's, at least, seven. Maybe eight. We'd better get a move on.

"We'll go as soon as Anne is finished examining you," Dahlia says. "She'll be here soon. How about we get you into the shower now, so you're ready for her?"

"Okay. Thank you, again. Thank you a million times," I say.

"We have your luggage packed," Rae adds. "I'm sure you'll want to take a quick glance to be sure we didn't miss anything."

"That shouldn't take long," I reply. "Did you get the things I set out to take to Rosemarie? Those are the most important items to pack."

"We did," Dahlia confirms. "Once Anne gives the okay, we can get on the road right away. Indie is ready to take us safely on our journey."

I agree, then Rae leaves the room while Dahlia helps me. Slowly and lovingly, she guides me to the shower and assists as needed with the tasks that I ought to be able to do for myself. I hate needing a caretaker. *Needy, needy, needy*, I am. This morning, though. I'm eager to do whatever will speed the process along. My destiny awaits. What's left of it, anyway.

Your time is running out.

By the time Nurse Anne arrives, I'm clean and dressed but tired again. I try not to make a big deal of it.

As I sit upright in my freshly-changed bed and Dahlia looks on, Anne does the usual checks of my temperature, my pulse, and my blood pressure, then she listens to my heart with her stethoscope. She asks me about my level of fatigue and shortness of breath, then she examines the swelling in my legs and feet. She notes the purple tinge beginning to develop on my feet, knees, and hands. None of the results are particularly good.

"Ruthie, what is your goal?" she asks pensively as she steps to the bottom of my big bed and leans her body against the footboard. Anne is a petite Chinese woman, and the king-sized bed dwarfs her.

I glance at Dahlia, who shrugs as if to say that I should be honest. I scratch my chin, pondering my answer. When I'm silent for a few moments, Dahlia jumps in. "Ruthie, Rae and I told Anne about your family circumstances, and she knows we plan to take you to New Orleans today. Don't feel like you have to start from the beginning," she says.

"That's good," I say sheepishly. "Anne, I knew you were off, and I didn't want to bother you with my personal drama."

Why do I feel like Anne is an authority figure who can stop me from leaving? She isn't, and she can't. She's a service provider I've hired to assist in my care. Nothing more.

"When I first started seeing you," Anne begins, ignoring my self-deprecating comment, "you didn't want to seek aggressive treatment for your heart condition. Is that still true? Or has your desire to reconcile with your daughter and meet your granddaughter changed your mind about things?"

I hadn't mentioned it to anyone, but this very question has been nagging me ever since I learned about Rosemarie. A little voice in the back of my mind tells me that perhaps I should change my tune and let doctors do all they can. What if they could somehow save me? What if I'm worth being saved?

"I don't know," I say, truthfully. "I've never wanted interventions that would leave me stuck without a decent quality of life. We're all going to die one day. The ideas of a feeding tube, being on a ventilator, or enduring grueling and risky surgeries have never appealed to me. Those extreme measures have always seemed so unnecessary."

"And now?" Anne asks.

She has an easy way about her. She's direct, and I know she'll stand beside me through anything that may come. She isn't afraid of sickness or death.

I look at Dahlia for guidance on how to respond, but she offers nothing but a kind smile. "This is all you, Ruthie. It's up to you and you alone. You decide. We will be here to support you, no matter what."

I sigh. "I guess my feelings on the topic might be changing. Maybe," I say. "I'm not ready to decide straightaway, though. I just want to get on the road while I have the strength. It feels like a million things could interfere with my ability to actually wrap my arms around my daughter and my granddaughter before I die … like that's a pie in the sky dream that has little chance of coming true."

Anne shifts her weight, but doesn't break eye contact. "I get that," she says. Her voice is strong and unwavering. She's determined to ask me the hard questions. "Is quality of life more important to you than living as long as possible?"

"It was," I say without hesitation. I've said it dozens of times, to everyone I know. Everyone I still keep in contact with, anyway. Anyone who would listen. I've been adamant about my wishes.

"And now?" Anne asks.

I look away, shifting my gaze to a spot on the floor where Dahlia has placed my slip-on shoes. All I have to do is put them on and walk to Rae's van, and a brand new chapter of my life begins.

Sure, I'm sad to leave my beautiful home and all the history it holds. I might never see it again. I'll probably never see it again. My gut knows that. Beyond these walls, though, in my daughter's world, the possibilities are endless. I've been here in this house—in this bed—for God knows how long. Even before my heart failed and I was put on hospice care, I spent far too much time lying around feeling sorry for myself. Feeling like my life was essentially over because I'd lost my Pete and my Meredith. Feeling like I had nothing left to live for.

And now?

"How should I feel?" I ask, my tone impatient. "Frankly, I'm overwhelmed by the recent opportunities I've been given. I don't know if they'll pan out. I'm well aware of how precarious my health is. I could get overheated and my heart could stop before we even make it to Birmingham. I see what's happening to my body as it deteriorates day by day. I know that I'm a mere shell of the healthy, vibrant person I once was. And if by some miracle I do make it to the New Orleans area unscathed, I'll need to figure out how to get Meredith to talk to me. I might have to help her from a distance, without actually being in her physical presence. None of it will be easy."

Anne's gaze is piercing. It's as if she's looking into the depths of my very soul. Maybe she is. Maybe that's what she's here to do. "Tell me about her," she says simply, her baggy blue scrubs taut against the footboard. I study the embroidered band at the neckline of her top and wonder if someone stitched the colorful medallion design by hand.

"Tell you about who?" I ask, even though I know full well who she's referring to.

She doesn't waver. She repositions one hand, leaning further in my direction as if to emphasize the seriousness of her inquiry. "Tell me about her," Anne says again.

She won't shrink. She won't let me shrink. I feel like I'm being taken to church. Or to the top of a mountain to meet a wise guru. Or something. This short interaction with Nurse Anne is turning out to be quite a life-changing experience.

A rush of emotion rises, and I tear up. Then, unceremoniously, something inside of me breaks. Anne's steady, forceful presence makes me want to confess all of my sins and wipe the slate clean. If not to Meredith, then to myself, at least. Maybe speaking my truth out loud would do my heart good—literally.

Sensing the shift in the room, Dahlia leans into the hall and motions for Rae to join us. I don't mind. In fact, I want her to be here for this discussion.

Without thinking, I go with it. I confess. I forge full speed ahead, unloading what's troubling me most. "Meredith doesn't know who her biological father is," I blurt.

I hear an audible gasp from Dahlia, but I don't look in her direction. Anne is unflinching. "Go on," she says. "Get it out."

"It's a long, complicated story. I did what I had to. I never meant to hurt anyone," I say.

"You knew all along?" Anne asks, her tone even.

I nod reluctantly, my heart pounding in my chest, yet feeling noticeably relieved all at the same time. "Yes. I knew all along," I confirm. "Meredith still doesn't know."

"That's a heavy burden to carry," Anne says. "You've carried it a long time."

I can tell Dahlia and Rae want to ask questions, but they're staying quiet. There's a palpable buzz in the room in response to my bombshell. I can only imagine how supercharged the energy would be if more people knew. If Meredith and Mitch knew.

"Her paternity isn't even the reason Meredith cut ties with me," I say. "If she can't forgive me for the rest, how will I ever break this news?"

Anne shifts her weight, pulling away from me, ever so slightly.

"You want to hear why she's upset with me, right?" I ask. "It's a reasonable question."

"Do you want to tell me why she's upset with you?" Anne replies, turning the tables.

Rae raises a finger in the air to insert herself into the conversation. "Those newspaper articles—" she begins.

Dahlia grabs her girlfriend's hand and pulls it swiftly downward, shooting her a stern look. "Leave it alone, Rae," she says in a tone that's more forceful than I'd expect from her.

I drop my head and stare at the shoes again. I could put them on and go. The action would be simple. Dahlia and Rae would help me, and we'd be gone. Do I really need this heart-to-heart chat with my hospice nurse? Deep down, I know that I do. So, I stay put as I summon the strength to continue baring my soul.

"Tell me about *her*," Anne implores. She turns and carefully picks up a framed photo from my shelves.

Inside the frame, a teenage Meredith smiles, her arm around Pete. The picture was taken on our front porch the night of Meredith's senior prom. She's dressed in a royal blue gown that's covered in sequins. The ballerina cut highlights her long, lean build. I remember thinking how suddenly and completely grown she looked that night. She didn't have a date, opting to attend the dance with a group of friends. I admired her for that. Back when I was a senior in high school, I would have been too embarrassed to attend the prom without a date on my arm. Times had certainly changed.

"She's the love and the joy of my life," I say through tears. "She and Pete. My everything."

"Pete is her dad?" Anne asks.

I nod, then stop abruptly. I close my eyes as I say the words. "Pete is my husband who died nearly twenty years ago. I loved him dearly. So did Meredith." I open my eyes again, ready to face what I must. "He's the man she *thinks* is her dad."

Anne bunches her mouth into a frown as she peers at the picture. "Ruthie, forgive me for being blunt, but Pete's dark."

"Yeah, so?" I ask. "He's the most handsome man I've

ever known. I think his dark, African-American skin was exquisite." I sound defensive. I can hear it in my own voice.

"He was handsome, yes," she replies. "I'm not criticizing. I'm just pointing out that Meredith's not dark like him. She has very light skin. Like yours."

"What are you getting at?" I ask. "What's that got to do with anything?"

Anne puckers her lips. "I can't help but wonder if Meredith already knows that Pete isn't her dad. I suppose she looks a little like him in certain ways, but his skin tone was just so dark. I don't think it's likely that he could father a child as light-skinned as Meredith. It's the way genetics work. There are certain inherited traits passed from parents to children. When there's a dark-skinned father and a light-skinned mother, the baby is likely to be a mix, somewhere in between the two skin tones." She pauses briefly, gauging my reaction. "Meredith looks like she has a Caucasian father. Did anyone ever mention it when she was growing up?"

I shrug. "At times, sure. Most people minded their own business. Meredith never asked questions, as far as I know. She has a long nose like her da—I mean, Pete," I correct. "They share a long, lean build. Long fingers, long facial features, and metabolisms that don't stop. Well, I should say that they *shared* those things. Past tense. When Pete was alive."

Anne pauses again, allowing me time to elaborate. I don't. I've said all I intend to about the subject.

"Ruthie," she says finally, replacing the frame on the shelf, "I sincerely hope you discuss this matter with

Meredith. Once you're gone, it will be too late for her to ask questions. Your daughter deserves the chance to ask questions." She walks around the side of the bed and pulls up a wingback chair from a corner of the room. "Not to mention, I've assisted hundreds of seriously ill patients in my time as a hospice nurse. I've seen up close how heart wrenching it is to carry a big secret like you do. My wish for you is to tell your daughter the truth. She deserves to know, and you'll feel so much better once you tell her."

I exhale, relieved that Anne seems to be allowing me a reprieve from her lining of questioning. "I'll take your words under advisement," I say. "It would mean a lot to set things right."

"Good," she replies. "I hope you'll give serious thought to how you want to be remembered. And I hope you do set things right."

From her mouth to God's ears.

"Does this mean you'll provide the okay for me to travel?" I ask.

She crosses her leg, hoisting it up and over a knee in one smooth movement. She laces her fingers together and places her hands in her lap. "I can't promise that you'll be comfortable, but you're free to travel, if you like," she says. "In fact, I'm happy to put in a referral to a hospice agency in Covington, Louisiana, where you're staying. They can provide continuity of care for long as you're in the area."

"Really?" I ask, my eyes lighting up. "That's great news! It makes me feel so much better. This way, they'll be available to evaluate me when I arrive, right? To make sure I'm pacing myself?"

"They can do that," Anne replies. "Hospice workers

are a caring bunch. I don't know anyone personally in Covington, but I'm happy to reach out to them. I'm sure they'll take good care of you."

I smile, then turn to Dahlia and Rae. "Did you hear that?" I ask. They nod reassuringly. "I hadn't even thought about the possibility of receiving hospice care down there."

"I'm glad, Ruthie," Dahlia says.

"Excellent news," Rae adds.

I lean over against one shoulder. I'm slumping as I grow more fatigued.

"Are you all right over there?" Anne asks.

"Oh, fine," I say, lifting my head. "I think I'll take a nap when we get into the van and on our way. I'll need my energy when we get there. I suspect this will be a marathon, not a sprint."

Anne nods and smiles politely. I'd like to wrap this up and get going, but I can tell she has more to discuss. "Ruthie," she begins, "do you have your legal affairs in order?"

Here we go. Your time is running out.

"You mean my will?" I ask.

"Your will, your advanced directive, and your durable healthcare power of attorney, for starters," Anne explains. "If you should need medical treatment while out of town, it will be important that those documents are complete and readily available to your traveling companions."

I glance at Dahlia and Rae. I've done the basic paperwork. I've been meaning to talk to them about it. I guess I've felt badly about leaning on them as much as I already do. I don't want to add the burden of making decisions about my care, should I be unable to decide for myself.

"That's a valid point," I say. "My lawyer has everything on file. I know I've been avoiding talking about the subject, but I promise to have a serious discussion with Dahlia and Rae so that I can iron out the details. Who knows? Maybe I'll reconcile with my daughter in time for her to help me make those decisions."

Anne peers at me. She doesn't have to say that my time is running out. I understand completely.

The three ladies remain silent as emotion overwhelms me. The image of my daughter, all grown up with a family of her own, pops into my head. I can see her standing at my bedside, conflicted and confused with little guidance as to how to navigate the carrying out of my final wishes. If I'm alert like I am now, that's one thing. But if I'm out of it and can't speak for myself, that's quite another. Tears wet my cheeks as the vision tugs at my heart.

Maybe I didn't think this through. Am I burdening my loved ones with more than they should be expected to handle?

"Sorry," I say as I use both palms to wipe my eyes. "Good thing I don't have any makeup on yet, because it would be running down my face right about now." I force a laugh, but it feels misplaced and inappropriate against the serious tone. No one laughs with me. "If only this dilapidated old body wasn't falling apart," I add. "What a useless piece of junk, huh?"

Anne leaps up, as if she's taken personal offense to my comments. I'm not sure I've ever seen her so animated. "Don't you dare say that in my presence," she says forcefully, grabbing my hand and shaking it. "Please, Ruthie, don't do it. That's not how you want things to end."

I'm taken aback. I was just blowing off steam. I didn't expect her to react so strongly. "Okay," I say, unsure how else to respond.

"I'm serious," she continues. "Your body—*this* body—is precious. This body has been with you all the days of your life."

"That's true," I say, but Anne isn't done.

A section of long black hair falls over her shoulder, framing her pretty face. She has so much life in her bright eyes. So much enthusiasm. So much wisdom. If I had to guess, I'd say she's somewhere around forty, although age is clearly just a number with her. Anne Li is an old soul.

"This body is the one your parents cradled when you were an infant," she says insistently. "They loved you, yes?"

I nod. "They did." My parents are both gone now, but I was close to them. They were wonderful parents to me. I couldn't have asked for any better.

"This body is the one that has carried you through the phases of your life like a loyal friend, yes?" she asks. "Didn't these legs walk you on many adventures? Into school, down the aisle when you married Pete, and back into school again, the second time as a proud mother escorting her beloved little girl? These legs are precious."

I'm getting the idea. She's exactly right. "When you put it like that," I say, "of course." I sniffle as the tears flow.

"These hands," she says, taking them both in hers

now. "They've held Pete's and Meredith's hands. They've done good work for you—in your business and for your family. These hands are precious."

"They sure are," Dahlia says, joining in. "Precious beyond measure."

"This body has worked for you—faithfully—for more than seven decades. What a gift!" Anne says. "What a blessing. What an honor."

I nod enthusiastically, feeling very different than I did a few minutes prior. I hate that I spoke so negatively about myself. I'm appreciating Anne's pep talk more than I can express. "Yes, you're exactly right," I say. "Thank you, Anne."

She leans forward, so close that she stops just inches from my face. Still holding my hand, she places it gently over my heart. "This heart," she says, "is precious beyond measure. It's ailing, yet it beats in your chest, even still. It has loved and lost, but it keeps beating. If you let it, I'll bet it will keep right on beating long enough for you to wrap your daughter and granddaughter in a loving embrace. Love yourself, and appreciate this magnificent body. Please, Ruthie. I beg you. Don't waste the time you have left thinking poorly of yourself. Countless others who have gone before you would give anything to be here now. *You're* here. Right now."

She's spot on. With that, there's nothing much left to say.

Anne goes over a few miscellaneous instructions for travel and promises to be in touch later in the day with a contact at the hospice in Covington. She helps carry the last of my luggage to Rae's van, then hugs me goodbye.

As we drive away, the question of how I want to be remembered firmly in mind, I watch my beautiful, beloved home of many years disappear into the rear view for what will likely be the last time.

There's no turning back now. My final chapter awaits.

14

—————

SCREECH

MEREDITH

New Orleans

"Meredith? Meredith? Can you hear me?"

A man's voice calls from somewhere in the distance. It's familiar, but I can't place it immediately.

I try to open my eyes, then squint against a bright light. I'm disoriented. I can't tell if it's daylight or dark. I don't know if I'm indoors or out. I feel like I should know these things. A sharp pain radiates from my ribcage, as if I've been kicked.

That can't be right, I think. *Who would kick me?*

"I'm here," I mumble, my voice a faint whisper. Although, maybe I imagined myself speaking. Maybe I didn't speak out loud at all.

"Meredith?" the man calls again. Whoever he is, he's insistent. "Meredith, wake up!"

I ball my face up, confused. The movement sends a

searing pain through my head. "Ouch!" I shout, the pain bringing me to.

The next thing I know, I'm being hoisted at the shoulder as a man embraces me. He pulls me against his chest and wet tears drip from his face to mine.

"Thank heavens you're okay," he says. "You had me scared to death there for a minute. I thought we might have lost you."

"Who's we?" I ask, my eyes fluttering open and closed.

The man laughs, and it's a big belly laugh that makes his whole body shake. I shake along with it as he clings to me.

Suddenly—and surprisingly—I feel like a young kid again. Like I'm in my room at my childhood home in Nashville, and my dad is trying to wake me from a bad dream. It feels like we've been through these motions many times—him calling my name and urging me to wake up while I'm somewhere far away, just out of reach. I can feel the love in the way he sticks with me. The way he keeps trying, until he finally pulls me back from the abyss.

"Dad?" I ask. "Is that you? Are you really here?"

I wasn't at home the day my dad died. I was away at college, in Savannah, Georgia, a full day's drive from the man I loved dearly and cherished with everything I am. I suppose I could have gotten on a plane when I received the news, and I could have been there in a few short hours. The airport seemed like too much of a hassle, though. When Mom called to tell me about the accident, I got into my little blue car and I drove. It was nearly dark as I gassed up and headed west on I-16. I'll never forget the way the taillights of the cars in front of me smeared and blurred, my vision clouded by tears. Sunset is still my least favorite time of day.

Before my beloved dad's life ended in what can only be described as a real-life nightmare, there was my predictable, comfortable childhood. Now, in this strange state of consciousness I find myself inhabiting—half awake, yet not quite asleep—my mind wants to take me back there. Perhaps to dwell in a time when things made sense. When bad things didn't happen. When I was safe.

I hear the familiar man again, and I feel myself being rocked like a baby. "Your mother is going to be so happy to hear that you're all right. She would have tanned my hide if I'd let anything happen to you," he mumbles, almost incoherently. He's choked up, crying and gasping for air as if his very existence depends on mine. As if he is personally invested in being sure I'm okay.

"Dad?" I try again, even though I know it doesn't add up.

There's no possible way my dad is alive, in the flesh. No way that he's cradling me in the here and now. He's been gone for years. Twenty years. In fact, he's been gone from my life almost as long as he was in it. I was barely twenty-two when he passed. I wasn't ready to face the world without him. Although, granted, I'm not sure I ever would have been ready. No one is ready to lose a fantastic dad like mine. Not at any age.

My senses returning slowly but surely, I can feel the familiar man's strong arms around my shoulders. They aren't my dad's arms. I know that now. But I seem to have a visceral memory of being held by this man. Somewhere, in the deep recesses of my subconscious mind, I think I remember being in his arms before.

"I've got to call your mother back," the man says. "Mine wasn't working earlier. I think someone jammed the signal near your rental house."

That triggers my short-term memory, and I recall being in our vacation rental property on Louisiana Avenue. I remember Hank and Becca being there with Silas, Rosemarie, and me, and I remember the dogs barking furiously when knocks sounded on the doors. The details are fuzzy, though.

I reach a hand to my face and find a warm, wet substance. Blood. Lots of it. It's sticky, crusted in some places and matted to strands of my long hair. It seems like I've been bleeding for a while.

The man lowers me down to rest on one of his outstretched arms, then a brilliant white light shines in my eyes. When he moves, I detect the faint yet unmistakable scent of cigarette smoke. I squirm at the sensory overload.

"Good. Pupils seem to be equal and reactive," he says, and I realize he's shining a flashlight into my eyes.

"What time is it?" I ask, rolling my shoulders as if I could shake this off somehow. I wonder why that's my first question now that I've realized my dad isn't here and this isn't just a bad dream. Other, better questions linger.

"You're okay," he says. I'm not sure if he's reassuring me or himself. He takes the bright light away, then wipes his eyes. "It's afternoon. Almost four. I've been searching for you for hours."

"Four?" That doesn't compute. We had dinner from

High Hat Cafe, which feels like just a little while ago. Evening dinner.

Keeping my head still, I look around and see that it is, in fact, daytime. The sun is high in the sky. It's hot, too. A typical May day in southern Louisiana. As if my senses are all coming back online at once, I begin to sweat.

"Don't try to move too much," the man says. "You've suffered serious injuries. We don't know what the situation is like … um, internally, that is."

Finally able to focus on my rescuer, I gaze up at his face. His features come into view and I recognize him. "Uncle Mitch?" I ask.

"Yes!" he replies with glee. "I'm here, Meredith. Everything is okay. You're okay. It's all going to be okay."

His reaction makes me wonder if this is a test that I've failed previously. Was I unable to recognize him before? "Okay," I say simply.

Okay is, apparently, the word of the hour.

I'm comforted to know that it's him. I'm also confused, though. Where am I? And how did Mitch get here?

"Let me think," he says as he wrinkles his brow. "What next?"

Being this close to him makes me realize just how much he's aged. Until I saw him at our Mandeville house the other morning—*was that yesterday or the day before?*—I hadn't seen him for a very long time. I don't recall exactly when, off the top of my aching head, but it was around the time my dad died.

Mom ran Uncle Mitch off, for some reason. She wouldn't tell me the details, but she was adamant that she didn't want me speaking to him. I suppose I was too overwhelmed with grief and stressed about finishing college to worry about it. It was all I could do to put one foot in front of the other and get through each day. Maybe I should have reached out to him. I doubt he deserved the cold shoulder he got from Mom.

That's one of her specialities, it seems. That and destroying our family. I suppose they go hand in hand together. Recklessness and ruin.

"Where am I?" I ask.

Mitch turns his attention back to me and gives my shoulder a gentle squeeze. "New Orleans, honey. We're in New Orleans."

Yeah, duh, I think, but I'm coherent enough to realize that would be a rude thing to say.

Hearing him call me honey stirs something inside. Did he call me that when I was a kid?

"Hold on a minute," he says, "while I figure out what to do with you. You need a doctor. And a hospital."

That doesn't make any sense. There's a disconnect in my mind, and I don't realize how badly I'm injured. I also don't remember what happened. "I'm in New Orleans," I say, "but I'm not in our house on Louisiana Avenue. Right?"

"That's right," Mitch confirms.

"Did I leave the house?"

Suddenly, concern for my husband and daughter hits me like a ton of bricks. Blood pounds in what feel like multiple sore spots throughout my body as panic sets in. "Mitch, my family. Silas and Rosemarie. Where are they?" I ask desperately. "Please, tell me they're safe."

"Well…"

He inhales sharply. That's not good.

"Tell me!" I shout, blood rushing to my head.

"Silas and Rosemarie are alive," he says. That gives me comfort and sounds alarm bells at the same time.

"Alive?" I ask. "Good, but why do you say it like that? *Alive.* Was there ever a question?"

"It's a long story, and I don't know it all," he stammers. "They're alive and safe. I know that much for sure. I saw them being carried out of the house with my own eyes."

I ball up a wad of his shirt with one fist and hold on tightly to steady myself. The thought of my husband and daughter being hurt sends a wave of nausea through me. I think I might vomit. I press my lips together in a feeble attempt to hold the contents of my stomach back. It's no use. I manage to turn my head just in time to avoid spewing all over poor Mitch. The vile liquid lands on a patch of bumpy blacktop below us.

"Sorry," I mumble as I wipe the corners of my mouth.

In slow motion, memories of being blackmailed float across my consciousness like tiny dancers. I remember the threats. The broken glass at our lakefront home. The guy at Hank's tavern. The people surrounding our vacation rental property. Hank and Silas' conversation about having a gun for protection.

The whole scenario seems preposterous. It seems like something that would happen to someone else. Not to me. Not to *us.* We're upstanding, law-abiding citizens. I remember Silas telling Rosemarie that we were targets because we have money. Is that true? I remember that there was more to it than that. More than I cared to share at the time.

I wonder how much Mitch knows. He used to be a cop. Maybe he has contacts on the local force.

"You say they were carried out of the house?" I ask.

"Yes. Well, sort of. Rosemarie walked. Silas was on a stretcher. They were both shaken up. When I got there …"

Mitch hems and haws far too long to suit me. "Out with it!" I say. I hope my voice sounds as forceful as I intend it to. I mean for him to know I'm serious.

He looks at me like he's about to tell me my puppy died. *Wait,* I think. *Did one of my puppies die?* My mind is struggling to keep up. I don't know what I don't know, and it's practically killing me.

"How about the dogs?" I ask. "Are they all okay? We have three of them—Alphie, Sara, and Calliope. Rosemarie loves them dearly. I don't know how she'd recover if something bad happened to any one of them."

The words are coming a little more easily now. Throwing up helped. I'm thinking more clearly.

"As far as I know, they're all fine," he says. "Becca had them closed in one of the bedrooms. I was most concerned about finding you."

"So, Becca is okay?"

"She is," he replies. "I believe she made it through unscathed. I'm not sure if it was dumb luck or what. She seemed fine."

His head drops and I can tell there's something else. Something big. But what? When it hits me, I gasp, the wind sucked out of my body. "Oh, no," I say. "Tell me I'm wrong. I have to be wrong. Tell me—"

Mitch nods solemnly. "I'm so sorry, Meredith."

Tears spring hot to my eyes. "Hank? Hank's dead? How can that be?"

"Yes," he confirms. "He was shot multiple times. His injuries were severe. By the time paramedics arrived, he had already lost too much blood."

"Shot?" I screech as tears stream down my face. My voice becomes alien. I don't recognize it. "No! He can't be gone. He was so vibrant. So alive. His daughter ... Oh, God. He wrote a letter to his daughter in the hopes of reconciling and reconnecting with her. He wanted me to read it. I have it in my purse."

Mitch's bottom lip protrudes like he might cry along with me. "It's terribly sad," he says softly, his arm still underneath my shoulders. "When accidents like this happen, well, they change entire lives. Our accident sure as hell changed mine."

I squint, unsure how to react. "Our accident?" I ask. "What accident would that be? Until the other day, I hadn't seen you for, what, two decades? I'm not sure there's an 'our' anything."

He looks confused, but proceeds to clarify. "Honey, I guess you haven't been privy to everything that's happened. It's all over now."

"What are you talking about?" I ask. "The accident where my dad was killed?"

Mitch helps me into an upright position, then moves in front of me. He squats, and I wonder how long his aging knees will be able to hold the stance. A quick glance around tells me that we're in some kind of alley or parking lot. There doesn't seem to be any traffic, so I stay put on the pavement.

"It's time you knew the truth, Meredith. The whole truth."

I take a deep breath, then wince as a shooting pain moves through my sore ribs. "Okay," I say, once I've recovered. "What would that be?"

Mitch looks pensive, sort of like a doctor who has to tell family members that a loved one has died. I wipe my cheeks with the back of my hands and wait.

"It's a lot to take in," he says. "Are you ready? Do you think you can handle it?"

I hear the sounds of a brass band in the distance. We must be somewhere near the French Quarter, which means I'm pretty far from our house on Louisiana Avenue. I put it out of my mind for the moment so that I can focus.

I'm still deciding whether I'm going to believe Mitch. It depends on what he tells me.

"I guess so," I reply. "I'm a grown ass woman. Not a scared kid anymore."

"All right. First of all," he says, "you're wrong about your mother. Very wrong. She and I have had our differences over the years, but Ruth Flores is a bonafide saint. There's no doubt where she's going when she leaves this world."

I look up at the sky and scoff at the absurdity. Maybe I should again entertain the idea that this is a bad dream. "Yeah, okay," I say. I realize that I sound like Rosemarie.

"I'm serious," he says. "She sacrificed herself. For you. For me."

"I find that hard to believe. She was having an affair, Mitch. She was cheating on Dad. That's why there was a scuffle. That's why a gun went off and killed Dad. It was all Mom's fault. If she hadn't been cheating …"

Mitch's expression remains calm and steady. He isn't surprised by any of what I'm saying. Which can only mean one thing. My face flushes hot with the realization. How did I miss it all these years?

"Honest to God, it was an accident," he says. "We didn't mean for anyone to get hurt."

"You?" I say, my tone scathing.

He nods. "I've loved your mother for most of my life. Did you know that I met her even before Pete did? We dated first. We loved each other first. When she and Pete got to know each other and started a romantic relationship, I backed away. But it isn't easy to walk away from love. It isn't that simple. Ruth and I drifted in and out of romantic love again and again. Pete knew that."

"Please," I say, emphasizing the vowels like Rosemarie does when she's irritated by me.

"I understand your skepticism, but it's the truth."

"Weren't you and my dad supposed to be best friends?" I ask. "What kind of friend has an affair with his bestie's wife?"

Mitch nods. "You're right. We were best friends. And we both fell in love with your mother." His knees have had enough, so he repositions and sits flat on the ground. "Sometimes," he continues, "life takes us on journeys we don't expect. Sometimes, things happen that we never mean to, and we end up feeling guilty when we shouldn't. Sort of like what happened with Hank today. It isn't your fault that he died. Not directly. You shouldn't feel guilty about your involvement in his death."

Ouch. That burns. I haven't had time to process Hank's death yet, let alone deal with any associated guilt. When did Mitch become so ruthless?

I'm angry, and I spit my words. "My sole focus in that situation is on finding Hank's daughter and giving her the letter he wrote. She needs to know what a good man her father was and how much he loved her. She needs to realize that there may have been misunderstandings and extenuating circumstances. That she had the wrong idea about him."

Mitch purses his lips and nods knowingly. "Exactly," he says. He pulls his phone out again, then cues up a video. He sighs heavily before handing the device to me and pushing play. "Brace yourself," he adds.

I stare at him for a few seconds, afraid to look at the screen. When I hear it, her voice pulls me.

"To whom it may concern," she says slowly. Her voice shakes, but it's her. It's my mom.

She looks so old and frail. Her eyes are dark and sunken, her hair is falling out, and her skin is paper thin. Seeing her like this feels like a dagger to my heart. I've always imagined my mom healthy and vibrant, out tending her garden and designing Nashville interiors, like she used to. Not once did it occur to me that she might be unwell. Not once did I think that we could run out of time to patch things up.

"What's wrong with her?" I ask as tears pool in my eyes. "She looks feeble. Is she sick?"

"Just watch," Mitch says.

He takes the liberty of giving my arm a gentle squeeze. I let him.

"This is Ruthie. Ruth Flores," she continues as she stares at me through the screen. It looks like she's riding in a vehicle. Road noise whizzes in the background and scenery races by. "I'm the wife of the late Peter Flores and mother of Meredith Flores Montgomery. I'm of sound mind. This is my dying confession."

I jam the pause button, tears instantly pouring down my face like a raging river. "What the fuck?" I ask, looking at Mitch indignantly. "Is it true? Is she really … dying?" My mind glosses over the confession part. I'm gutted by the news that she's dying.

He nods slowly. "I'm sorry. It's true. Ruth—though she goes by Ruthie now—is in end stage heart failure. She's been in hospice care for a few months. That's why she reached out to me and asked me to track you down. She wants to make peace before she goes."

I shake my head. I can hardly believe this. "So, that's why you watched my house? And talked to my daughter?"

"That's right," Mitch replies. "I was learning about you at first. Figuring out if you might be willing to have a conversation with your mom. Then I found out that you were in trouble. I couldn't stand by idly and watch once I knew there was real danger involved."

That, I understand. "I know. I'm glad you didn't." I wipe my cheeks again with the back of one hand.

"Keep watching," he urges. "It's all there."

I exhale sharply, still feeling the pain in my ribs. I steel myself, then push play again. My mom smiles warmly before she continues. It almost feels like she's smiling just for me. A pang of mixed emotion swells in my throat.

"Twenty years ago, my husband, Peter Flores, died when a gun accidentally went off in the driveway of our home in the Nashville suburb of Brentwood, Tennessee," Mom says into the camera. "Pete had been involved in a scuffle with an unidentified man. After an investigation, I was arrested and tried for his murder. I was ultimately acquitted. The man was never identified. The gun was never recovered."

She stops and coughs, one shaky hand covering her mouth haphazardly. It takes a minute for her to catch her breath as coughing turns into sputtering and wheezing. "Oh, Mom," I say. "You don't have to do this."

Mitch nods, urging me to keep watching. "Police and news outlets are already in possession of the footage," he says quietly.

"I had a daughter in college at that time," she continues. "She had lost a parent, and she needed me. Given that situation, I did what I had to. I withheld pertinent information from the authorities to protect my reputation and livelihood." She pauses, as if waiting for gasps from a crowd, only she isn't in front of one.

"You," I say to Mitch as it all begins to make perfect sense. "You're the unidentified man, aren't you? You were there. She's protecting you."

"And you, like I said," he adds. "Keep watching."

"I was holding the gun when it went off," Mom says. "It was an accident, but it was my finger on the trigger. I can prove it." She coughs again, then places a hand on her chest to steady herself. "There's an old well on my property about fifty feet from the back of the house," she continues. "I tossed the gun into the well, then I covered it with ready mix concrete. If the police look, they'll find it there. Ballistics will confirm that the bullets pulled from my husband's body are a match."

"Why now?" I ask out loud, already knowing the answer.

As if she's responding directly to my question, she explains. "I'm voluntarily coming forward with this information now because it's been brought to my attention that someone who knows the truth is blackmailing my daughter, Meredith, and threatening her young family. This person has demanded an outrageous amount of money in exchange for their silence. And, in an effort to be loyal, my daughter has, apparently, been wrangling with this unscrupulous person for quite some time. Today, with this confession, I've taken away their leverage. Now the world knows the truth, and my daughter can be left alone to live her life in peace."

I pause the video and look at Mitch. "How did she know?" I ask. "I didn't tell a soul. I *purposely* didn't tell a soul. I was going to pay them to make it go away. I was just stringing them along while I figured out what to tell Silas when that much money disappeared."

He smiles now, proud of Mom. Maybe I'm proud, too.

"Magdalena," he says. "She went to college with your mom. When I found you, then told Ruth that I thought you were in danger, she put that big brain of hers into overdrive. She got lucky, too, reconnecting with Magdalena and realizing that the woman was already working in your home on your renovation project. It didn't take much convincing for Ruth to get Magdalena on her side."

"And Magdalena … what?"

"Spied on you," he confirms. "Sort of, but I wouldn't look at it that way. Magdalena secured the information your mom needed to neutralize the threat. The guy who was threatening you has been arrested. The truth is out. Nothing and no one related to this incident can come back to haunt you ever again."

"Wow," I say. "I mean, I'm glad my family is safe. I don't know how I feel about the rest."

Mitch smiles again. "Your mom decided that there was no better way to get eyes and ears inside your home than to enlist the help of the professionals who'd been hired to make renovations. It's a brilliant plan, if you ask me. She used her knowledge of the design world to think creatively about who had the necessary access. You have to admit, she got results lightning fast."

"That, she did," I reply.

Mitch all out laughs now. He's proud. "Your mom wanted a name for the initiative. She called it Southern Charm Society. I have no idea where she got the name, but she wanted us to call it that. She suggested there could be a secret society of designers in the future, utilized to investigate and resolve issues based on the unique access they have. You've got to love her feistiness. I sure do."

"You knew?" I ask. "About Southern Charm Society?"

He nods. "I did. It's only been—what?—two days. Not

long at all. I would have told you, I promise. But that's water under the bridge now. The plan worked. That crazy old broad pulled it off. Just in the knick of time, too."

"Wait," I say, alarmed. "What do you mean by that?"

He shrugs and his big shoulders heave. "Well, look at how I found you. You're hurt. You could have been killed. Your family could have been killed."

"You helped save us," I say, my frustration and animosity leaving me.

"I might have had a little something to do with making the connections, but it was Ruth who made it happen. She's your hero."

I smile. It's the first time I've smiled while thinking about my mom in a very long time. I can't even remember how long. I reach for the pendant around my neck. It's still there, untouched by whoever roughed me up. I'm glad I have it.

"Uncle Mitch?" I ask.

"Yeah?"

"There's more. Isn't there?"

He shoves a hand through his hair. "Like what?"

"Like, why is she protecting you? I get that you two loved each other, but it was an accident," I say. "I get the feeling there's a bigger reason that Mom wants to be absolutely certain you aren't charged with murder. What is it?"

Reluctantly, he takes his phone back and thumbs to another video, then hands it to me. Mom's face appears again. She looks even weaker and more fragile. I can instantly tell that this time, she's speaking only to me.

"Meredith, my baby girl," she begins with a smile. "I

hope you know how sorry I am for everything that's happened. I wanted to be a good mom to you. I love you dearly—more than life itself. Since you're a mom now, I hope that you understand."

I break into tears. Big, voluminous tears that soak my face. I try to wipe them with the backs of my hands, but there's no possible way to keep up. "Oh, Mom," I whisper.

"There's something that I have to tell you," she continues, "and I fear you'll be angry with me for not telling you sooner. I hope that, someday, you can forgive me. I'm dying, and well, I need to die with a clear conscience. So, here it goes."

Mitch puts a hand on my shoulder as if he might need to keep me from crumpling into a puddle on the ground when I hear the news. He, clearly, already knows what she's going to say.

Mom coughs and sputters again, then finally, she blurts it out. "Pete isn't your biological father. I'm so sorry." I breathe deeply as I take this news in. "Mitch Weller is. He's your biological dad. Pete knew all along."

I shake my head and close my eyes. I'd suspected, but I hadn't wanted to face it. "You knew, too," I say softly.

"Don't be mad at Mitch, honey, please," Mom says, anticipating my reaction. "He's a good man who will be a bright spot in your life after I'm gone. He can tell you stories from the old days. Let him love you, for Pete and for me. He'll have to love you enough for all three of us. Be good, my baby girl. Remember the good times. Of those, we had many. I'll be watching over you and my granddaughter. I love you, forever. Goodbye."

The video ends, and Mom's face sits frozen with a

peaceful smile. I can tell she feels better having gotten that off her conscience.

Overwhelmed by emotion, I burst into tears and throw myself against Mitch's broad chest. I'm too moved to let silly grievances keep me from a parent any longer. I love Mitch. I always have. He kisses the top of my head, and it feels right.

"I guess I have to stop calling you uncle now," I say with a laugh.

He laughs, too. "That's probably wise."

He holds me, here on the pavement in a New Orleans alley, for what feels like an eternity. I think through as much of this as I can process at once, and Mitch waits. He doesn't push me. He simply waits. He's a good dad.

"Mitch?" I ask.

"Yeah?"

"I want to go to Nashville," I say. "To visit Mom. I want to take Silas and Rosemarie so they can meet her and see where I grew up. Will you join us?"

He pulls back and looks me in the eye. "Honey, you don't have to travel to Nashville. Ruth is on her way here. To get to you."

A new flood of tears emerges. "She is? How? Where?" I'm a blubbering mess. I can hardly speak.

"Friends are driving her—Dahlia and Rae," Mitch explains. "I spoke with Rae a little while ago. Ruth has slept almost the entire way. She isn't doing well, and the trip is taking an even greater toll than they expected. They had planned to drive it over two or three days, but with her sleeping so much and given her health, well, they pushed through and kept going. They'll arrive at a cottage they rented in Covington in about an hour."

"An hour?" I say, pushing myself up to a standing position. I'm lightheaded, but I can stand. "We have to go. Right away."

"I know," he says. "My car is here. I'll drive you. You seem okay. I think the doctor can wait until you've had a chance to see your mom."

"Silas and Rosemarie?" I ask. "They have to meet her. They just have to."

"I know," he says again. "We'll call them on the way."

I nod, then we walk together, arm in arm, united and ready to face what's next.

15

QUICKEN

RUTHIE

New Orleans

It was a bright, clear Louisiana evening when I took my last breath. I was surrounded by loved ones, including my daughter and granddaughter, who were holding my hands.

I'd felt the life draining from me over the course of months, then weeks, then days, the pace intensifying with no sign of slowing down. I was afraid, at first, but ultimately began to focus on where I was going rather than what I was leaving behind.

There were amends to make, and I was lucky enough to have experienced a grace that allowed me to set things right. I don't know whether it was sheer chance or divine intervention, but either way, I couldn't be any more grateful.

Today, as Dahlia and Rae drove me, my ailing heart seized and sputtered. I could tell that it was running on fumes. I was running on fumes. They fussed over me, lovingly, and they offered to take me for medical treatment along the way. I refused, knowing deep down that my video confession would be enough to set my daughter free and that—thanks to dear old Mitch and the power of the truth—she'd finally understand. I had to get to her to say goodbye.

On the wings of angels, we drove hour after hour, until we reached the place where I would touch my loves and then take my rest.

When I crossed over, bursting out of my body with a joy like stepping into a cool swimming pool on a warm day, Pete was there to greet me. A beautiful garden framed with pearlescent white light came into view, and there he was, standing in an archway.

"There you are," he said as he stretched out his strong arms to envelope me.

"Here I am," I replied as I moved close and nuzzled into his warm, familiar neck. "I hope I didn't keep you waiting."

"My precious love," he replied, smiling as wide as the Mississippi, "I'd wait forever for you. Welcome home."

THE END.

———

Like *Southern Charm Society*? Read Kelly Utt's other books. Visit kellyutt.com.

ABOUT THE AUTHOR

Kelly Utt writes emotional, pulse-pounding suspense, family saga, and women's fiction novels. The stakes are high. The twists and turns will keep you on the edge of your seat.

Kelly was raised by a dad who would read a book, ask her to read it, too, and then insist they discuss it together, igniting her passion for life's big questions. That passion is often reflected in her novels, giving them a depth which leaves readers wanting more and thinking about her stories long after the last lines are read.

Kelly holds a Bachelor's degree in psychology from the

University of Tennessee, Knoxville and she studied graduate-level interactive media and communications at Quinnipiac University.

She lives in Nashville, Tennessee with her husband and sons. She also writes supernatural thrillers with one of her sons as the combined pen name Christopher Kelly.

www.kellyutt.com

www.christopherkellybooks.com